DIVE

ADELE GRIFFIN

HYPERION BOOKS

FOR CHILDREN

NEW YORK

For information address Hyperion Books for Children,
114 Fifth Avenue, New York, New York 10011-5690.
First Edition
1 3 5 7 9 10 8 6 4 2
Printed in the United States of America
Library of Congress Cataloging-in-Publication Data
Griffin, Adele.
Dive/Adele Griffin.—1st ed.
p. cm.
Summary: Young Ben finds that he is happy in the stable life
provided by his stepfather despite his uncertain relationship with
his moody and troubled stepbrother and his mother's growing
restlessness in her new marriage.
ISBN 0-7868-0440-8 (trade: alk. paper)0-7868-2389-5 (lib.: alk. paper)
[1. Stepfamilies—Fiction. 2. Family problems—Fiction.
3. Emotional problems—Fiction. 4. Interpersonal relations—Fiction.
5. Parent and child—Fiction.] I. Title.
PZ7.G881325Di 1999
[Fic]-dc21   98-51080

Also by Adele Griffin

Rainy Season

Split Just Right

Sons of Liberty

The Other Shepards

You would have called her a fruit-cake.

Why do you want to get into it with that fruitcake? Your laugh sticking to the words.

The alarm clock winks 12:00, but my watch reads ten to six. Downstairs, Lyle is unloading the dishwasher and humming and clearing his throat. My fingers rub the dots of the phone mouthpiece; from inside I hear the tin lady's voice.

If you'd like to make a call . . .

Mallory isn't in the phone book, which

is why I got her number memorized.

She's unlisted, Lyle had told me after her first session, pie-eyed because Lyle himself would never keep hid from people. Next thing he said was about her being famous.

Famous? How, famous?

On TV famous, he answered, and he rolled up onto his toes, a hand knobbed in each pants pocket, he lifted up and then he pitched back on his heels. Channel Five on the weekend news. We'll watch her some-time.

So I looked at him funny, because you know Lyle, he won't let words tip out of his mouth for the sake of hearing them drop. Sure, I said, and when Lyle went up-stairs I opened the folder he'd left on the kitchen desk and read her index card.

She lived in the city, so even her area code was different. I memorized it straight off. I like secrets, especially ones that don't belong to me.

If you need help, hang up and then dial your operator.

I blow out my breath and I punch in her numbers.

"Hello?" Her voice is scared since it's too early for calls.

"Mallory?"

"Bennett? Is that you?"

"Yeah, Ben." Even after six months, she forgets about how I'm not a Bennett.

"What's wrong?"

"It's Dustin. He got hurt."

"What happened?" Next thing I hear is the flap of covers as she squirms herself up.

"We don't know exactly. He was out on the beach, he'd been climbing some rocks and he fell. He broke his arm or his shoulder, messed himself up pretty bad. My mom called around midnight. He's in the hospital. Our plane's at seven-ten."

"How bad is *pretty* bad?"

For the third time I tell her we don't know. Then it sounds like a dog got hold of the phone from the way Mallory's snuffle-breathing. I know she's trying to think if I should put Lyle on.

"Where's Lyle? Would he want me to go, too?"

My turn to sniff and huff. "He's downstairs."

"Which airline?"

3

I tell her, and on the other end I hear the knock-around movements of Mallory out of bed, gangling through her room. I picture it like in a hotel. Slippery pillows and long curtains and no mess.

"Ben, buddy?" Lyle calls from the kitchen. "Let's get moving, guy."

"See you," I whisper, and then the phone's back together in one piece like it never happened.

Why you want to get into it with that fruitcake? you ask inside my head. Her and her glimmery eyelids, her clicky shoes. What do you get out of it?

Because you'd never put a person to use unless you had to. You'd call Mallory an extra, somebody who might lean back if she got leaned on.

I can handle it myself, is what you'd say. I got it, thanks anyhow.

No matter how much use another person might be.

Although there's times I try seeing through your crooked view on the world, unlike you, I don't mind a little leaning. I don't mind Mallory's concern.

When I go downstairs, I see Lyle's got

my cereal ready, with a folded napkin and the milk in a jug.

"Juice first. Long day ahead of us."

I think maybe I should say something about phoning Mallory. Then I figure if she shows up at all, she'll be able to explain her reasons for coming with us better than I ever could.

So instead I lift my glass and drink, one long slow sip to the bottom.

It was Lyle who figured out about me and juice, back when I was seven and Mom and me had just moved in with him.

Ben's an honest-to-God pain-in-the-you-know-where when he wakes up, she told Lyle, after I'd got in a tussle with her about combing my hair or washing up or whatever show-off thing she'd been gunning me to do before breakfast, just to prove to Lyle how good she raised me. Then she called me Son of Frankenstein, making her monster face of a tooth-grille smile and popped-up eyebrows. Her acting foolish was another show-off thing for Lyle, but it didn't strike me funny since the joke was on my real dad's name—Frank—and missing him still felt like mud on my heart.

Maybe it's low blood sugar, Lyle answered. He reached over and poured me a long glass of orange juice to the brim.

Drink it all down at once, Lyle said. Some people need a hit of juice to get started.

And some people just need to get hit, you said. You were thirteen, six and one quarter years older than me, but even then I knew you shouldn't have been so smart-mouth, and I was surprised that nobody talked you back.

Instead, your insult spun out like a lasso over all us three, since you were equal mad at everybody—at Mom, for moving in with Lyle; at Lyle, for letting her; and at me, since I came attached to Mom. It was the fact of me more than the who of me that irked you, I figured. I hoped.

Then Mom laughed and blew a circle of smoke from her breakfast cigarette. We watched it halo the table, and your own mouth O'ed in copy pretending like the smoke had come from you. Then Mom reached across and flicked your ear, which caught you by surprise.

Wise apple, she said. Kiss your girl-friend with that mouth?

You slid your eyes to the corners and pulled a kind of smile to one side of your mouth.

If I did, I wouldn't say, you answered. How do you do those?

So Mom passed you the rest of her cigarette in spite of Lyle's dark look, his mumbling, Well, now, Gina, I don't think. . . . And she gave you some pointers, letting you hack and spit while you tried to make rings. Meantime, I lifted my glass of orange juice and glubbed it all the way down to the end without stopping.

And Lyle was right, it perked me up not bad.

Sun is beginning to sift through the moth colors of morning once we hit the road. We listen to all-news radio and the Zoo before switching to country. I wait for the music to ease Lyle's mood before asking him.

"What else did Mom tell you?"

"Not so much. She's upset."

"Will he recognize us? Be awake and all?"

"I couldn't tell you. It was hard to get a straight answer out of your mother."

The side of Lyle's face is fiercer than

the front, where he looks like those olden-days paintings of Jesus, if Jesus had worn tortoiseshell glasses and flannel shirts. From the side, though, Lyle's face is carved and fixed as furniture. From the side, the words *your mother* sound bad, like she's my fault.

"She ask about me?" I'm careful to talk low in my stomach, to make the question sound less jiggly than how it feels coming out.

Lyle's mouth seals, from the side it is straight as a shelf, and he shakes his head no because he can't lie, but he doesn't want to say the truth. His hands prove the scatter of his thoughts; one big fist clumped on twelve instead of spaced to three and nine on the steering wheel, and he forgot to wear the Weatherman gloves I gave him for Father's Day.

"Did you pack light clothes? It's in the seventies out there."

"Yeah." I nod, though I can't recall this minute what's in my cargo overnight.

"And a toothbrush?"

"Uh-huh." Except I know definitely I forgot that, toothbrushes are hard to remember even on a planned-out trip, being as how they're in a whole different room from where you're packing. My answers seem to make Lyle more restful, though. He slides his hands to eleven and one.

"Twenty-three minutes," he says, and we both eye the dashboard clock, because once Lyle sets a time, it's a contest to see if he can get us there on his prediction. Lyle says the only rule is not to speed, that the challenge is in making it legal.

Close inside that same time you said some people should just get hit was when you showed me your knife. You called me into your room specially. I was pretty happy because I'd never got used to your silent treatment, and I took whatever bone you threw to be friends.

It wasn't much of a knife, its plastic handle roughed up from too many spins in the dishwasher and a blade that couldn't cut free a slice of salami. How I remember it at all is because you kept it hid under your mattress like a criminal.

Who you gonna hurt with that? I asked, thinking maybe you were warning me, giving me an hour to collect my stuff and make my getaway.

Your face was dark from lifting up the mattress. You let it drop and slid yourself slow to the floor to lie flat on your back with your eyes on the ceiling and thumbs drumming your chest. I don't have plans for hurtin' no one, you said, dropping off the *g* like in the movies or the South. Not this week, anyhow.

Who you goin' to rob then? I asked.

Nothin' to rob in this neighborhood, everyone here's got the same of every-thing.

Hey, I know what. . . . And here I'd crouched low, shuffling my feet closer to you, my hands rubbing together so you'd know I was your ally. Hey, I know what you can do. You can take that knife and chop off someone's legs, like a frog's legs, maybe.

It was probably one of the worst things I ever said out loud. I got sweaty in my armpits just developing the picture of a legless frog, and I didn't believe you would

1 3

do it, but I was using bribe words. I was telling you I was tougher than you might have judged. That I wasn't planning to rat on your mattress knife.

There was a time I'd have said anything, done anything to impress you.

That's obscene, you answered. You have major problems, runt. Sick in the head.

You watched the ceiling while you talked, and you kept staring at it after the words were through. Even when I said I was just kidding and sor-ry, and what did obscene mean, anyway?—still you didn't look at me. And I knew you'd forgot about me, even as I stood right there in front of you, wishing I'd have said something different, something better, that would have caught your attention or made you bust up laughing.

But I never had those kinds of good words on me, and you always turned away from me, sooner or later, to go back inside your private thoughts.

So I retreated down to the kitchen to find my own knife, or something else important that I could hide in my room and maybe show you. The only thing I felt okay filching was a cheese slicer, which I kept under my mattress but then finally had to chuck in the school Dumpster when I couldn't stand to hear Lyle ask one more time where it had got to.

It takes us twenty-seven minutes, four minutes overtime, which I mind as a first hint of things falling apart. Lyle acts like he doesn't care, but there's extra juice in how he slams the trunk after pulling out our bags. In movies it's clear when something's about to go bad, either by the music or the camera zooming in on some unlucky thing, like a missing-eye doll or a broken window or lightning. In real life you've got to be on lookout.

Mallory's car is red, with a top that hums down when you press a button, but I don't know what exact type it is since cars aren't my thing. We steer up the parking ramps and I keep guessing every red one is hers, but when we get inside the airport and check-in and find our gate and Mallory still hasn't shown up, I start to think that she might have reconsidered us.

Lyle buys a newspaper and coffee and a glass bottle of apple juice for me, which I don't want, so instead I peel off the juice wrapper and fold it into a Slice. As I'm making it, I talk under my voice, pretending I'm an air-force aerodynamics model instructor giving orders.

"Good morning, men. As you know, the Slice is a classic dart model. It is excellent for distance and preciseness. Please pay attention and I will now inform you of my secret method of construction. First. Smooth your paper so it does not include any creases, this is for navigational reasons. Then. Fold in half. Then. Go like this, making into two triangles on each side, like a mirror. Flip over and fold up the opposite way for your rudder. Open in half and crease the wingtips. Recrease the rudder. Make sure wings join nose in as sharp a Y shape as you can get. Done. Perfect. Class dismissed."

My Slice comes out not bad. It's slick-shiny gold-and-red combat colors, but it feels too light and I wish I had a paper clip to weight the nose. I want to send it on a test flight across the lounge, and I check on Lyle to see if he's watching me. He's not. He is looking bull's-eye at the space ahead, and I know before I turn in her direction that it's Mallory.

"Bennett called," she says in an apologyish voice once she gets into talking distance. Lyle already has hopped to his feet. They curl their arms tight around each other. "I'm on standby, but they said it shouldn't be a problem."

"What about the station? It's a bad idea for you to miss work." Lyle takes a step back from Mallory. He usually goes a little screwy when people want to help him, but it comes off rude. Lyle has more practice with being the helper and the other way around is not true to his nature.

"Work can wait," Mallory says, flicking her hands. Her nail polish is a between color you'd get if you melted up tinsel with raspberry jam, and her mouth's a perfect sparkle-berry matchup. She wears her famous-lady sunglasses so I can't see if she's got glimmery eyes, but I bet yes because everything else on her—dark pants, skinny sweater, gold necklace, gold earrings, clicky shoes—has been perfectly put together. If Mallory was an airplane model, she'd be tough to assemble, like an Ages 12 & Up.

"I had a fairly uninformative conversation with Gina," says Lyle, and I think he does an eye crossover to me, meaning *more about that in private*, because all Mallory says is "Ahhh," and then she asks Lyle if he'll come to check-in with her and see about other ways to get her on the plane. Lyle tells me to stay put and guard the carry-ons.

From the back, you'd say they look weird together. Lyle's clothes make a map of wrinkles and Mallory is head-to-toe perfect. Lyle's straight brown hair needs cutting, it bends inside his jacket collar, but Mallory's fuzzy brown hair is short enough that you can see exactly how her skull is shaped. She is like our across-the-street neighbor Mr. Englander's garden, so spruced that you feel like a stray dog cringing for the kick if you get too near. Me personally, I wouldn't want to spend the time on myself, but then I'm not on TV.

I watch them all the way up to the counter, and I see how when Lyle talks, Mallory keeps her chin moving up and down to show she's listening, and when Mallory talks, Lyle cups his outside ear to block off the airport noises.

Fruitcake or not, I bet you would have admitted she was the perfect one to call, if you'd spared it the thought.

You considered all of Lyle's clients fruitcakes anyway, but the way I saw it some were more fruity than others. There are the people who go to Lyle because they're nervous to talk in public and they need some pointers. To them, Lyle's a kind of coach who stands on the sidelines and calls out stuff about projection and pitch. Then there are people who go to Lyle because they're scared of everything, and talking in public is just one more item to check off a long list of fears. To them, Lyle's like one of those playground dads, following

21

behind his kid with one hand fanned close not quite touching the back of a neck or belt loop, braced to catch their fall.

Aquaman probably stood somewhere between those two categories, but for a long time he was your favorite fruitcake. You showed me how, wedged inside the second-floor-bathroom sheets-and-towels cupboard, you could hear right through the wall into Lyle's office. We sat with our knees buckled against the closed door and sucked quiet fingerfuls of peanut butter from a jar that we passed back and forth as we listened.

Lyle started all his clients on relaxation breathing, which was too hard to hear, followed by consonant and vowel warm-ups. Aquaman's were the best. We liked to listen to him go, *Charge, cheetah, charge!* or *Pi-pi-pi-pi-pickle! Ki-ki-ki-ki-kitty!* Maybe since he looked too solid for the robin chirp of his voice. Maybe since we'd sneaked a look at his index-card fear (he'd got voted head of the PTA, and now every couple of weeks he had to make speeches to a bunch of parents and teachers). All I know for certain was that Aquaman got

you loopy. I'd have to put my head between my knees so as not to catch your
wild, glow-in-the-dark smile. One look
and I knew I'd upchuck every laugh and
mouthful of peanut butter trapped inside
me.

Dad's clients are smackpuppies, you'd
groan after Aquaman, moist in the face
and fumbling for Lyle's check, had been
shown downstairs and out the front door.
A guy that big actually thinks he'll pee his
pants because he has to stand up and talk
to a bunch of teachers? That is sad, man.
That is so sad.

Sad, man, I repeated as I shook my
head in agreement, following you into the
family room, where we put on Super Nintendo. We didn't look at Lyle when he came
in some minutes later and asked if we'd
been eavesdropping on him and Aquaman.

This is my business, boys. Mr. Aquient
relies on my discretion. It is an implicit,
confidential agreement that the two of you
are violating.

Lyle's lecture voice could give you a
feeling kind of like a stomach wedgie,
but I'd learned to copy you, keeping my

attention on the TV screen no matter how much I wanted to say sorry. Show it some respect, okay, guys? Ben, Dustin, are you listening to me?

Uh-huh, you answered for both of us. And we kept calm as clocks until Lyle was all the way downstairs before you said, for both of us, Shheeez.

"I'm all set." Mallory is standing over me, fanning her plane ticket in my face. "Wake up, Bennett. You're in a daze. They found me a seat. We're boarding."

"Why do you always call me Bennett?" I ask. "When it's just Ben."

"Because I prefer Bennett," she says. Her full answer.

I check my Swiss Army watch that Mom sent me this past birthday when I turned eleven. I'd buckled it on before we left home, changing it from the special de-signed left-handed watch that Lyle gave me the birthday before. The left-handed watch is better, since the windup stem is on the left side and the strap buckles on the right, so technically it's easier for me to work. But I figure Mom will like to see her gift in use.

"Do we get another breakfast?" I ask Lyle as we join the line of people shuffling onto the plane. Lyle keeps a lobster-claw hand on my shoulder like he thinks I'll break loose.

"Should," he answers. We squeeze up to wave at Mallory, already settled in her good seat in the front of the plane.

"Hey, no fair," I say.

"These malinky legs need stretching space," she answers. The guy sitting next to her laughs, a sound that wants everybody to know how terrific it is to be in the expensive seats, and his smiled-up cheeks squeeze into two shiny pink eggs.

"Lyle's legs are longer'n yours."

"Turn around and heave ho, sport-model," says Lyle. "This isn't a cruise. We'll be off in four hours."

"I'll come visit later," says Mallory. She slips off her sunglasses and closes her eyes, the gold on her eyelids glimmers like fish skin. Eggcheeks gives her the once-over, then stares ahead and darts her sideways eyes. He's recognized her as the lady from Channel Five. Sometimes it's cool, she told me once, but mostly it gets you stuck in small-talk quicksand. Best to keep your sunglasses on or your eyes shut.

Lyle lobster-claws me all the way to seats 37E and 37F deep in the back of the plane. "If this explodes, we're all of us done for," I say. "Did you know the back and front are statistical crispers? Heads and tails, the most dangerous parts of a plane."

But Lyle mutters something about how the plane won't explode because it would be too much bad luck in one week. His answer makes me feel quiet, and I keep my tongue still until he asks why I phoned Mallory.

"Are you mad?"

"Don't answer a question with a question."

"It was up to her to come. Besides."

"Besides what?"

Besides, you need someone for when you see Mom, I almost said, but I didn't

2 7

want to get into it with Lyle. So instead I say, "Besides, Mallory's nice," which works a little smile into the middle of Lyle's stiff-edges face.

"She's nice to be here with us," he agrees. "She's missing work, but she says they can spare her for the next couple of days." I know Lyle's talking out loud to persuade himself.

"If Mallory says it, she means it," I remind him.

The pilot's voice comes on. He introduces himself and talks about the plane ride, then he says I guess the same stuff in Spanish, a long strip of words like *burra-burra-caracha-day*, and I wish I knew Spanish.

After he's done, the TV screens show an instructions movie about what to do if we sink or catch fire. I'd already seen it last year, when Lyle took me to Dolphin World. So this time I yawn and budge around to show the other people how I'd been on a plane before and I already know about the secret gizmos above and under my seat. A plane is boring, like sitting in a too-crowded movie theater except for you're strapped in seat belts and there's no popcorn. First time Lyle took me on one was a big disappointment.

"Don't kick," says Lyle, clapping a hand on my knee. "Store the energy until after we land."

"Okay."

"We have to save our strength for helping Dustin, right? He needs us now."

"Right." Which isn't true, because I never knew someone who had less need for people than you. Lyle's got to have that one figured out by now, but I guess he has a hard time seeing himself any other way than as the guy somebody else might need.

When Lyle started dating Mom, you told me you'd thought she was a client, scared of the peep of her own voice and hunting down Lyle for bravery lessons. Showed how little you knew about her. By the time she met Lyle, Mom was already employed as a telemarketer for an insurance company, selling accidental-death-and-dismemberment policies. This much for a leg, a little less for an arm, and a stash of cash to your next of kin if you packed up and died. Any person selling D & D insurance over the phone can't afford to be shy, or there goes your commission. Mom never had trouble with talking, no need for Lyle's help or his book, *Speaking to Save Yourself*. The fact of it was she met Lyle by pure chance on Valentine's Day in the Stop & Shop, both of them looking for oven cleaner.

We'd moved into town after Mom left Dad, which turned out to be for the last time, only I didn't know it then. There'd been a week of driving far, far away from him, then another week in a Budget Lodge motel, until she found us a one-bedroom sublet in the King Plaza Complex.

It's not much, but it does the job, Mom said. And we've seen worse, right? Now that I've got a steady paycheck, I think it's time to plant some roots.

I said I thought so, too, although I was betting we'd hook up with Dad soon enough. He always found us, especially after Mom broke down and called him to tell him where we were. Meantime, I liked the apartment. The lamps, stereo, and TV were all programmed to one handheld remote control. The sofa was a pullout for me, with cushions made from bogus tiger and leopard skin. There was even a stack of naked-lady coasters in the coffee table drawer. Mom said typical slime-dog bachelor pad. She acted to all our apartment neighbors like she'd lived better Before, that the King Plaza was a step down.

It seemed to be only a small while after we'd settled in that I started hearing Lyle's name. First Mom was talking on the phone to Grammie about the nice man from the Stop & Shop, then next thing I knew I was being baby-sat by pickle-breath Mrs. Roberts from across the hall while Mom met Lyle for dinner and a movie. Then a twelve-red-roses delivery, then me writing *Lial called* on the message pad while Mom was in the basement doing laundry. He talked low and rumbly, different from the soft static of Dad's voice.

I still can picture the first time we pulled up in your driveway. I had my fingers on the door handle, ready to jump because Mom had smelled up the car with her hairspray. You and Lyle were standing on the front lawn, tossing a baseball. Snow was heaped up on the sidewalk, but the day was warm, good catching weather.

When I got out of the car, the first thing Lyle said to me was that my glove was next to the lamppost. I looked and there it was, a Wilson original, camouflaged on the brown winter grass and smelling like spring.

All yours, Lyle said.

I barely thanked him and had it tried on before you pitched the ball at me, aiming straight for my face, and when I blocked for the catch, the force snapped my wrist back quick and painful.

Whoa, nice play, Lyle called to me, with a smile to water down what you did. But then his eyes strayed to you, unhappy. Lyle doesn't push it but he wants things to go down easy. That's why he's good at his job. He can't stand thinking about people getting mucked up in the complication of themselves.

Mom was wearing her pink dress and there was no right place for her to sit and watch us, so Lyle had to quit playing to keep her company.

You boys practice with each other, he said, while we fix lunch. But as soon as Lyle took Mom's arm, you squirmed your hand out of your mitt and tagged along behind them into the house. So then I had to go, too, although I'd rather have stayed outside in the good air. There was no yard at the King Plaza, and the desk guy yelled if you ran in the lobby.

This is my living room, that's a picture of my mom, over there's my dining room. Upstairs is my bedroom and my work space. In back's my kitchen. My mom hand-painted those flowers on the kitchen table. That's my mom's scarf on the peg by the back door.

You were pointing to everything at once and talking squeaky out-of-breath like a girl.

Where's your mom now? I asked, confused and wondering if my own mom was breaking the law, trying to steal a husband while the wife was out at work or grocery shopping. I wouldn't have put a move like that past Mom, she never said no to a little sneakiness, like returning clothes to the store after wearing them with the price tags tucked in, or pretending like she'd never ordered that second or third glass of wine whenever we went out to a restaurant.

You got up in my face and told me in that same girl voice that your mom died from breast cancer two years ago. I had heard about breast cancer and my box turtle, Fast-Slow, had died last year, but I did not want to talk about these wrong things—breasts, cancer, or dying—with you, an older kid I hardly knew.

Can I see your room? I asked.

I'll show you her, you said. There's pictures.

So while Lyle and Mom made sandwiches and lemonade in the kitchen, we shared a space on the living room couch, a photo album parted over our laps, while you made me hear the story of your mom. You wouldn't stop about it, how sometimes she used a wheelchair and how she lost her hair from the medicine, and how, right before she died, you all went on a cruise to Bermuda. It was the most perfect week of your entire life, you said. You even saw a thresher shark.

I must have sat there a billion years, watching your grimy fingernail as it dragged over squares of ultrablue sky or a suntanned Lyle, but mostly of your too-skinny mom with her head wound in a scarf and her arms spiraled around a littler version of you.

This is boring, I said after a while.

Leave then. Who wants you here—you or your fruitcake mom? You shut the book and centered it carefully on the coffee table. My dad knows some ladies, but my mom is number one. She's number one, he tells me all the time. No one can take her place. Your mom's not so good-looking, either. Her ears stick out.

I pushed my nose into my baseball glove and smelled and hoped for a terrible thing to say back.

My dad could whip your dad in a fight.

Anyone could whip my dad in a fight, you said. Even I could. Maybe one day I will.

It wasn't the answer I expected. I want to go now, I said.

Go. Who's stopping you?

Her ears do not stick out.

Nobody asked you to come here. My mom talks to me at night from Eternity and she said, Don't let strangers in our house, especially not in the dining room with the silver candlesticks, because they could be robbers.

So I punched you where it hurt. I knew, since I was getting beat up a lot in my new school. A good six inches above the belly button, square between the ribs. You doubled over, then jumped, catching my leg as I made a coward's break for the kitchen. Then you leaped and rolled on top of me, grinding your elbow into my chest until I thought my heart would rupture. I was pounding the floor with my heels and wheezing for Mom, and with her and Lyle only a sprint away, you knew your time was almost up. Still, there were a few seconds left where you could have punched back, jammed some fingers, maybe yanked a joint out of its socket.

Instead you mashed my cheeks tight between your thumb and fingers, then pulled my head rough to the side and dipped your face low to my ear to whisper words damp and hard enough to flood shivers through my body.

You'll never be my brother.

The plane lifts into the air. My ears pop and Lyle passes me a stick of gum. He says he bought it at the airport shop along with my apple juice. Lyle is a think-aheader.

"Mal's probably just starting her champagne and shrimp cocktail." I try to get a look.

"Sit down, Ben. The seat belt sign is on. They'll put you in airplane custody if you can't follow directions."

"You're lying."

Lyle shakes his head. "I'll have to report you to the GCA."

"Whatever." I fiddle for my seat belt. When I was younger, Lyle had me believing that the GCA was a real place, like a courthouse. You were the one who told me there was no such thing as the Good Citizens' Alliance.

That's Dad's phony-baloney, you told me. Only in his dreams is there a place like that. He'd elect himself president. President Citizen.

Even after four years, Lyle won't let on that the GCA's a joke.

A plane lady wheels down her cart, asking if anyone wants a beverage. I call out, "Grape pop!" before Lyle can intercept my choice with more juice. Lyle asks for coffee but he doesn't drink it, just watches it and stirs it with a plastic straw.

"Not since Thanksgiving, right? Five months, it's been," he says.

"That's about right." I know what Lyle means. It's been five months since we saw Mom and you. It should have been four months, but you both were on a boat this past Christmas, on a scuba-diving trip along with your new girlfriend, Melanie, and some people from Mom's job at the vet

3 9

clinic. So Mom had pushed up your visit to Thanksgiving, except for Lyle made it to be like Christmas, baking his special ginger-bread and buying presents, and he didn't schedule any clients for the whole week.

"Mom brought that free turkey," I say.

"Free-range, not free," Lyle tells me. "He seemed good, wouldn't you say?"

"Dustin? Yeah, he was good."

"He got tall. He was always going to be tall."

Which kind of gets me, since it's look-ing like I'm not going to be tall like you or like Lyle. Runt, you used to remind me. Or Big Ben, for a joke.

"His hair covered his ears," I remind Lyle. "You didn't like it that way, but he said it was the style there. Sure isn't the style here, huh?"

"Mmm." Lyle closes his eyes. His hands rest under his head. He is twisting off each part of Thanksgiving and then putting all the pieces back together. Soon he will ask me a question about a wrong piece. Sure enough, a few minutes later, he opens his eyes.

"Did you think he was too skinny?"

My mind works on that one. Then I say something about how living at the beach, I guess a person'd get skinny. Running and swimming all the time. "Dustin told us he was always outside," I remember. "He bought that surfboard. He said he was on the beach night and day."

"Mm-hmm," Lyle answers. "He's loved water since he was a baby. Probably we should have taken more vacations upstate, near the lake. That might have been—"

"Even Mom looked skinny, for her."

"Well, but that's from smoking," Lyle says. "A pack-a-day habit destroys you. Appetite, lungs, metabolism. If you're not smarter with your own health when it comes time to make those choices, then I must have raised you wrong."

Only lately Lyle has let slip a few bad things about Mom. Lyle's words usually line up straight on a balance beam of caution. Could be it's because I'm getting older, and he feels more man-to-man. Could be because by now he figures Mom isn't coming back to us. Which is something I knew the day she left.

Mom moved herself and me into your house pretty quick after our first visit. I knew you weren't one hundred percent happy about it, but I wasn't the one making decisions. All I could try to do was to keep out of your way during your gloomy fits; let you eat the last of the taco chips or watch whatever you wanted on TV, even if I'd got to the remote first.

Besides, it soon came plain to see that your moods depended more on what was churned up inside you than what happened around you, which made you hard to predict. One minute you were letting Mom dance you around the kitchen with the stereo turned up past the 40 dB line, the next thing we'd find you sitting in the dark on the back stoop, telling us no, you didn't feel like eating dinner and no, you didn't want to come inside. Lyle told me and Mom that your moodiness had been a part of you since always. He said this in a sort of emptied-out voice, like that lost way people comment on how the universe is too big for measuring, or how many hours a person sleeps in one lifetime.

Meantime, Mom never seemed to be anything except for excited. On the phone to Grammie, she went on and on about whirlwinds and getting swept off her feet, like Lyle was a twister running her down. Most likely there should have been more waiting time, but I guess when two people don't want to be alone, there's nothing to stop them from crashing into each other.

Mom dialed-a-lawyer to start the divorce from Dad, who finally showed up late that spring, wearing some extra pounds around his middle and smelling too strong of ketchup and coffee. He took me to lunch at the doughnut shop and promised to call me every week and maybe take me out to see the Space Station that summer, just us guys. I told him that the Space Station was a great idea, and I watched Dad's car all the way down the block after he dropped me off, but he had been promising me the Space Station since I was four years old. Dad's leaving was mud on my heart, but it was also a feeling I'd got comfortable with. Through all the years I remember of Mom and him, there was never a time when one or the other wasn't threatening to go.

Until Lyle's, I'd been everywhere and lived nowhere. I'd camped out in apartments and trailers and mobiles and sometimes with Grammie, who's way up north and lets me eat corn chips and red hots for dinner. I'd sat in passenger seats, slept in lobbies, waited on doorsteps, played at neighbors' houses—it didn't matter where I spent my time so long as I stayed Out of the Way while Mom and Dad messed up or straightened out things between them.

But I'd never been part of a real house, with a newspaper delivered to the front lawn and yellow tomatoes growing out back. So in my mind, you were the lucky one. You'd had the paper and tomatoes your whole life, and the way I saw it, Lyle had rooms to spare. Even if you were mad that I was budging in, I didn't concern myself about it, not really. Not enough to say I didn't want your work space for my very own bedroom. Not enough to stop myself from scraping *BEN* into the trunk of your backyard maple. Not enough not to list your address as mine when I started scouts camp that summer.

Your moods were nothing, in exchange for what I got.

On Lyle's instruction, you cleared out your posters from the walls of your work space, along with your comics collection and Spider-Man rug, and we weren't better than two strangers on the third floor, no more than a bathroom and the silence between us. Even at Mom and Lyle's engagement party, you played that game of always stepping out of the room I walked into.

You hated me fierce all through that first year, and when I remembered to, I hated you back.

4 5

Mallory doesn't come to visit us until the movie is starting. She crouches next to Lyle's seat and they whisper together. I lean hard over my armrest, but I can't hear their secrets. The lady sitting on the window side has fallen asleep and her breath is crawling too close on my ears and neck. I hold my shoulder up to my ear, then I zip my jacket all the way to my chin. Then I nudge the lady with my arm to redirect her breath. The first time doesn't work so I nudge harder and she wakes up with a gasp noise.

"Would you please mind your space?" she says in a whisper that has slurp in it.

"You were breathing on me," I answer, in my regular voice. Lyle turns and with one hand he pushes my chest deep into the seat back.

"Is my son making trouble?" he asks.

"He woke me up," huffs Slurpwhisper. "He elbowed me."

"I'm very sorry about that. Ben and I will make certain it won't happen again," says Lyle. They talk over me like I'm not even here.

I stretch back my neck and roll my eyes and go, "Shheeez."

"Come on, Ben," Lyle says. "What would Ms. Faunce think? At the last parent-teacher conference, she told me you'd been maturing in leaps and bounds." He takes his hand off my chest. Even though it didn't really hurt, I go, "Oww!" and start a wild coughing fit. Leaps and bounds—like I'm some dumb rabbit. Ever since that conference, Lyle'd been way over-talking those leaps and bounds, even though old Ms. Faunce is the type who'd put in a good word for any kid.

47

"Bennett," Mallory whispers. "Do you want to trade? If you give me your word that you'll behave, I'll let you."

"Trade for the rich-people seats?" I ask, leaning over Lyle, who is looking at Mallory like she just lost her mind.

"Right." She nods at me slowly. "But you have to promise you'll be a man. Promise me no horsing around up there. No elbowing, no nonsense."

"I promise, I promise," I say.

"I'll tell the flight attendant Lyle and I want to talk privately, and that's why we're trading."

"Okay, yeah."

She pats Lyle's arm and is back in a minute with one of the plane ladies.

"Nice meeting you," I say to Slurp-whisper as I stand up. She opens one eye at me and frowns.

Mallory leads me to her big spaceship seat and makes me promise her again. So I promise her again. Then the plane lady comes over with earphones and a blanket. I move back the seat as far as it can go, set my earphones to a good music station, and settle in.

Inside my mind swims up a picture of you, the way I imagine how you are now, asleep in a germless steel bed and wearing one of those tie-back napkin nightshirts that hospitals use for clothes.

Ben, if you want to use my old room as your work space, you can have it, you tell me in pretend. 'Cause I'm never coming home again.

But Lyle's sad, I answer you. He needs you back. Even if I don't, not really, not anymore.

But you're way better than me at being Lyle's kid, you say.

"You think?" I ask out loud, and my own real live voice freaks me; not just because of how it bursts out by accident, but because it sounds way too happy.

Boy am I a jerk.

I look over at my new neighbor, Eggcheeks, to see if he'd heard me talking, but he's rolled over on his chin and snoring. I take care not to elbow him. I know how to keep a promise.

It wasn't until after I saw you dive that my hate feelings about you changed some.

The town pool and tennis club had opened for the summer, my first summer at Lyle's, and one day we all went over for swimming. I was feeling not-so-good with the day at first, on account of Mom. She was wearing her new pink two-piece. Pink is her favorite color, but like everything else, Mom took it to the extreme. The rest of the mothers had on one-piecers, some of them with attached lettuce-leaf skirts. Mom seemed to have a spotlight shining on her stomach, from the way people's eyes kept straying to it.

Lyle wasn't bothered. He liked Mom's uncarefulness. She was different from his clients, who wrote Lyle thank-you notes about how they finally stood up and spoke their piece in front of the boss or auditorium or wedding banquet, after reading his book. Mom had no shyness of the Other People, no worry about how she expressed herself in public.

Still, I bet there were better expressions than giving the whole town a whopping eyeful of your stomach whether they liked it or not.

Dustin's going to dive for us, I hope, Lyle said, starting in on you right away. You were walking apart, a couple of steps ahead and to the side, pretending like you weren't with us.

I don't know about that, you answered without turning around. My back's stiff. Which was your inside-out way of letting Lyle know you were still mad about mowing the lawn. It was your weekend chore, and while you never talked against it directly, your comments circled in shadowy

5 1

rings around your main complaint.

One dive, Lyle persisted.

For me, added Mom.

You kept walking, your hand reached around massaging your back.

When Lyle said you could dive better than anyone in town, I had my suspicions. I thought Lyle was making an angle on the positive. "An Angle on the Positive" is the title of chapter three in his book, about how important it is to concentrate on the good parts of yourself so that you can face your audience with brave eyes and a steady voice. I figured you needed those positive angles more than I did. You were the one Lyle whispered to Mom about, the one who had taken to sleeping in a tent in the middle of your room and hanging around with a bunch of kids who wore black T-shirts printed with skulls and dripping-blood words.

Maybe he's forgotten how to swim, Mom said, teasing.

That's not going to work, Gina, you answered.

The afternoon loafed on, with Mom and Lyle standing waist-high in the shallow end water, talking and leaning their backs against the wall, and me doing jackknives with a kid I knew from my class who had decided to stop beating me up now that second grade was almost over. His friendliness made me feel good. I took it as a sign of an easier time in school next year.

You spread a towel over the warm concrete along the pool edge and watched the other kids jumping and diving off the low, middle, and high dives. Your legs were crossed at the ankle and wedged up to your chest, your arms hugged your shins, and your nose dug into the space between your knees. You stayed like that all afternoon, until the sun had quit warming the top of the water and families were packing up to go home.

Are we leaving now? I asked, after my new friend had been called back and hauled away by his family. My fingers are getting peely, see?

In a little while, Mom said. We're waiting to see if Dustin wants to go in.

Lyle sneaked a look at you.

Is he gonna dive? I asked.

Only if he wants to, Lyle answered.

You waited. I'd seen you do this before, hold the same position for so long it was like the real you had gone somewhere else, leaving your body parked behind like an idling car. You waited until Mom finally had climbed out of the pool and disappeared into the changing cabana, and Lyle was collecting our books and tanning lotions. I was at the snack center, in line for a drink of water at the fountain. I probably wasn't supposed to have seen you either, except I was watching. Even as far back as then, I had a hunch of you that you didn't especially appreciate.

It happened pretty sudden. You spouted up from your towel and started running like a short-distance hurdler, fists like hammers, back-tucked elbows, puppet knees. You speeded down the side of the pool and then began to scale the ladder, two rungs at a time. Even as I scooted out of my place in line, running to get a better look, you were already out on the edge of the high-dive board, whipping it up and down in long slinging bounces.

Then you leaped clear, and your body caught the air the way a kite catches wind.

The slide of my own sucked-in breath was the only sound to go with my picture of you as I watched you fold into a smooth hand-toe touch before you stretched and tensed and dropped like a dart aimed clean through the center of the world. You hardly bubbled the surface of the water as you shot beneath it. Inside a crazy second, I wondered if you had figured out a way to disappear.

You surfaced to the sound of people clapping, me included. It was the best dive I had ever seen off TV. Lyle was clapping too, heavy hard claps, and yelling, Atta boy, Dustin! Way to go, kiddo! but his eyes were also straining past you to the cabanas. Mom had missed your dive completely.

But this was your inside-out way of getting back at Lyle.

My eyes groggy-open to the glass and echoes of another airport. This one is too hot and I'm stuffy inside my clothes.

"Lyle, Lyle, Lyle," I say. "I'm awake. Put me down, I'm not a kid."

Lyle stops and drops me to my feet. "The only person I know who can sleep through a plane landing," he says.

I take off my jacket. "Are we close by the hospital?" I ask.

"Not exactly," says Lyle. "It's about another hour by car."

"We'll need to rent one after we claim

our bags," Mallory says. "What kind are you thinking, Bennett?"

"Red drop-top," I say. "Like your other one."

"That's unnecessary," Lyle grumbles. "We don't need that."

"Skinflint." Mallory is joking, but she's right. Lyle's a pincher. He keeps a giant water cooler full of loose change in his office at home. Once it fills to the top, he takes it to the bank. The money he gets in exchange he puts into his retirement account, which he calls his rainy-day plan. Lyle's as ready as Noah for a rainy day.

Lyle uses a pay phone to call the hospital. His expression doesn't show a hint of the news he's getting, but he gives a quick thumbs-up when he catches me staring at him.

"They say Dustin's stable," Lyle says when he gets off. "But listen to this—he'd been moved this morning from *critical*. Gina didn't even tell me he was admitted to critical because of some head trauma. She didn't even tell me!" Lyle can't seem to stop repeating this all different ways. "She didn't even *tell* me. She didn't *even tell* me."

"But now he's stable," Mallory says. She makes the surface of her voice all smooth, like to remind Lyle of what the word stable means.

Lyle catches one of his hands in Mallory's and the other one in mine. "I'm very glad you two are here," Lyle says. "Thank you for being here with me."

For a minute we stand linked and quiet while other airport people drag past us, mulepacked with luggage and snack foods.

After we collect our stuff off the bag-wheely machine, we head to the car-rental booth at the other end of the airport. Mallory asks for a midsize red convertible four-door. She gets mad when the car lady hands the forms to Lyle to sign.

"I'm paying and I'm driving," Mallory announces. I can tell she's using Lyle's chapter two: "Your Vocal Focus." Her voice is so big that other people turn.

The lady gives the key to Mallory and apologizes, but it's too late, Mallory's energized. As soon as we're out in the car lot, she starts in on her speech.

"I've earned my own salary and paid

my own way since I was sixteen years old. More than half my life spent as a working woman. To still be faced with that kind of prejudice really gets me where I live."

"Ah, she's a dumb teenager," Lyle says.

"No excuse for ignorance," Mallory answers. "No excuse." She wears her chin and mouth pulled high.

We stay quiet because there's no arguing with Mallory when she is taking her stand against Ignorance. Once I asked her what was hardest: being famous, being black, or being pretty. When she frowned at me I thought she was mad, but then she rubbed the top of my head like you'd pet a dog, and she told me she was living fine with all of it. She told me it was other people's opinions about her that got to be tiresome.

The weather is warm and the sun presses pinwheels through my eyelids. Mallory forgets her bad mood as soon as the guy drives the car around. Cars aren't my thing, but I can tell this one is top quality.

"Mal, I don't know," Lyle starts.

"When it comes to the selection and steering of the automobile," she says, "I'm in the driver's seat. And if we get ticketed, I'll pay."

Mallory is a whole different type of driver from Lyle. She wouldn't ever set a time of arrival or think that the challenge is in keeping it legal. She zoops down the top and vv-vrooms the engine, rolls the stick shift through its gears, and cruises back and forth between lanes so many times that soon we don't have any car friends left on the highway.

From where I sit, Lyle looks unbendable. He rests a hand exactly the same way on each knee knob. From the front he must be a sight; it's like taking Abraham Lincoln out for a spin. Mallory turns to him and goes, "Whoo-haaa!" a couple of times, to try to spur him into the mood. I join in with a "Whoo-eee!" but neither type of whoo takes effect.

"Tell us where we're going," Mallory shouts through the wind, and so Lyle pulls out the map the ignorant teenager car-rental lady gave him. He seems to relax as he slides his fingers over the roads that lead to the hospital. Mallory knows how to get Lyle sidetracked.

I feel the crunch of my juice-wrapper Slice tucked inside my jacket pocket. Soon as I pull it out, the wind's grabbed it backward from my hands. I turn around and it's a firefly on the highway before it crazy-catches another direction and then it's gone, sucked underneath the hood of the car behind us. I keep watching, hoping that it might snap back to me or pop out the other side, but it doesn't.

Lyle figured out about me and airplane models, even when Mom said I probably didn't have the patience for them. But she was wrong and he was right, which was becoming a pattern, so far as I saw it. Lyle said from the minute he saw my first paper airplane, a Swallowdive that unfolded into a birthday card for Mom, he thought I had more complicated designs inside me. He said my brain was right for holding three dimensions.

The first Sunday Lyle came back from the hardware store with a model, I thought it looked too hard, which gets me smiling now, since it was cake. An F-14 Navy Tom Cat, only eight separate pieces. Lyle said he'd help, but the model was mainly my project. He put down newspaper on the kitchen table and read me the instructions while I built it myself. After the glue dried, I painted it gunmetal with U.S. and French flag decals. Then Lyle showed me how to string clear-varnish–coated twine through the holes in the wings. We hung the Tom Cat from a long tack Lyle hammered into a corner of my bedroom.

The next Sunday, Lyle brought back a Desert Patrol Vehicle. It was an Ages 9–11, except for I had only just turned eight.

This one's all yours, bud, he said. I have confidence you can do it.

It took me a week to finish, and I had a hard time with the rubber cement, nonsoluble, which means it never washed off. My hands smelled like glue all day at school, reminding me of how much I needed to come home.

When the DPV was done, Lyle said I was almost a pro.

Lyle strung it and tacked it up on the

opposite corner of the room. At bedtime my decals glowed better than the night-light I'd pitched in the trash after you made fun of it. The only thing out of place was how my planes looked against your shadowy Spider-Men crawling up the sides of the walls.

You used to be real into Spidey, with the fake web-spinner and Halloween costume and everything, and your mom had wallpapered your work space special. After I took over the room, you told me it was baby wallpaper only good for pee-wee runts like me. I think you said that since there was nothing either of us could do about me sharing the room with Spider-Man. Except for I didn't even want him.

My complaint about the wallpaper knew to stay put, because it was too close to getting into it with you about your mom and your work space. So I kept quiet until my third model, a World War II B-17 Allied Bomber with two 300-pound bombs and thirty one-caliber machine guns, plus a detachable driver and two gunners. The box picture showed a man building it alongside the kid, like a warning of how tough it was to assemble. Only I did it alone. It took almost two weeks to finish, and Lyle said hands down it was the best workmanship of the three. Maybe I was feeling extra proud, but after Lyle hung it, I couldn't help by accident saying a small bad thing about Spider-Man.

I know it's not how you see your room, Ben, Lyle answered, but let's wait awhile. Let me wait for a good time to talk to Dustin. Changes are hard on him.

Yeah okay, I said out loud, but in my head I wasn't perfectly agreeing.

It wasn't too long after, though, that I came home from school to see bald walls and my bedroom furniture pushed into the middle of my room. My three models had been unhooked and were lined up careful on my bookshelf. I found the long strips of Spider-Man squashed in a pail in the bathroom.

Surprise! called Lyle when I came downstairs. We're giving your room a remodeling, so to speak. Okay by you?

Sure, I answered. Sure, it's okay. Thanks, Lyle.

Thank Dustin when you see him, Lyle said. He green-lighted the idea.

Thanks, Dustin, I said to you later at dinner. You shrugged and looked over at Lyle. Your face was sealed quiet over your thoughts.

That weekend our bathroom was full of brushes and paint cans labeled Prussian/Semi-Gloss. I stood in the door-way and watched while Lyle painted all four walls the smooth blue of clear skies. I told Lyle he was the coolest and I meant it.

Only later that week Spider-Man was back, taped in crooked sheets to the out-side of your door. The strips were bumpy from being in the pail, and the design didn't match up anymore. Some places Spidey's foot was coming out of his waist or he looked like he had two heads, and the paper was flopping over at the top. I didn't know what to do except for tell Lyle first thing that maybe painting your work space wasn't such a green light idea, after all. I saw him cup a hand on your shoulder before you left for school.

Whatever you and Lyle said was noth-ing that turned into my business, but

Spider-Man stayed on your door. Although you never spoke direct to me about it, I minded it as a private sign of how much I'd wrecked your house.

Motels stink, I guess since they remind me of Before. This one is not bad, I've slept in worse. Still.

Mallory is acting Very Special, as Lyle puts it. At the check-in desk, she is asking the lady too many questions. The lady has a worried face, and her lips twitch from all the questions Mallory keeps throwing her.

"Is there continental breakfast?"

"Do you have a workout room?"

"Are feather pillows available?"

And when Liptwitch says, "Oh my, wish I could help you with that but no,"

Mallory repeats, "No breakfast? No feather pillows, really? Hmm, that certainly is less convenient than I might have expected."

"They've got a pool," I speak up.

"No room service at all?" Mallory asks. Liptwitch looks even more worried as she twitches no. People don't like to disappoint Mallory; nobody wants a rotten stare from a good-looking face. I know this firsthand from last year when Jennifer Gold cut me a stare to freeze hell over after I budged her in fire drill. We're next to each other in sixth-grade homeroom this year, and so far I've managed never to turn in her direction on account of not wanting to come under that stare again. Jennifer Gold is too much of a looker for me to survive it twice.

Lyle says he'll be back with the bags at the same time Mallory says we should try to find another motel. Their words jumble together and then they're both quiet.

"It's got a pool," I repeat, and amazingly that settles it. Mallory gets the room keys, one for her, one for Lyle and me, as Lyle heads out to the car for the bags.

Me, I need to run. My plane nap, the strong sun, our fast car, and no school have put me in a flow of energy. I can't even snap my mind over the fact that soon I'll be seeing you and Mom.

Outside, I spy a paved walkway bending along to the back of the motel. So I go. My sneakers are new and they make me run fast. I round the corner and there's just rubble, no more walkway, and I'm heading for a gravel-dirt hill. I aim for the top. Lyle's calling my name, a sound soft as a curl of smoke in the hot air and just as easy to ignore.

The hill is steep and I'm sweating. I pull off my sweater and knot it around my waist. Slowing down, but I keep pushing, digging my toes into the hill to keep my balance. I'm feeling charged with blood, oxygen, muscles. Feeling good to move move move on instant brain command.

I go and I go.

The top of the hill is higher up than it looked, but it's in my mind now to keep running, because once I'm up there I'll be the highest part of the hill, the owner of it.

What Lyle calls undependable, Mom calls free. She and Dad raised me loose, without much attention to rules, theirs or anybody else's. Always I was the kid who needed extra days to hand in his field-trip permission slip, because Dad and Mom kept forgetting to sign it. The kid who came home with teachers' notes explaining how cut-off shorts or jeans with holes weren't acceptable attire and please make a note of it. The last kid to be picked up from a birthday party. Always it was me. Always me.

71

But Lyle's house has rules. They are simple and they never change. Make your bed. Finish your homework. Unload the dishwasher. If I miss a rule, I pay for it. No television. No phone calls. No Super Nintendo.

Mom didn't come into Lyle's house with any rules, and you figured that out quick. You were always tugging her over to your side, which got easier when the problems with Mom and Lyle began to widen the spaces between their good times together.

Since day one there had been little shakes, like Mom telling Lyle he was too strict and who cared if you stayed out past your curfew or if you skipped gym? But I always count the night of Crash by Force as the place in time that cracked and broke the ground dividing you from Lyle, with me standing on Lyle's side and Mom next to you on the other.

It started with Lyle not letting you go because Tuesday night was a school night. I actually didn't hear him say those words. You repeated them to me after you'd slammed upstairs and banged into my room, to talk and pace it out.

He won't let me go. I already paid for these tickets and the concert starts in five hours. How am I going to tell Daphne?

Couldn't you resell them? I asked.

No. Yeah, but that's not the point. Daphne might even break up with me over this. It's so unfair. Every other kid in my class is going. I need to talk to Gina.

You slammed back downstairs and waited for Mom, and I know she must have taken to your side, because dinner that night was just lots of scraping forks and knives, with Lyle's face starched into stiff edges and Mom chain-smoking at the table, even though Lyle had made a rule about no cigarettes during meals.

After I went back upstairs, I heard you in your room on the computer, and I figured you were sending raving-mad e-mails to your friends. I got ready for bed thinking you were still in your room. So when Lyle came up a while later and switched on my light and asked where you were, I was truthfully stumped.

He's not in his room?

Not since I checked ten seconds ago. I

think he took the out-the-window, down-the-drainpipe route. Gina's MIA too. She said she was going to the drugstore, but that was about a hour ago. Lyle's chin was tucked down, he was talking at the floor, and it hit me that he was embarrassed. That he felt dumb and tricked.

I don't get it, I said, and I didn't, but Lyle must have. I followed him into his study, where he called Daphne's house. Daphne's mom told him that Mom and Dustin had picked up Daphne on the way to Crash by Force.

She said she was glad for the adult supervision, Lyle told me after he got off the phone, laughing a little; a sound that I hated because I knew he was laughing at himself, at the joke on him. Then he said go back to bed, that everything would be straightened out by morning, and he went down to the kitchen to make coffee and read and wait. I crawled upstairs but I couldn't sleep, I just lay there bug-eyed and waiting and waiting for you and Mom to come home.

But I must have dozed off anyhow, because voices startled my eyes open. Mom's voice especially. It was late, past midnight, and when I scooted down to the kitchen everybody seemed a lot more awake than me. Lyle was sitting at the table drinking coffee, not saying a word, just watching Mom, who talked enough for two, all blah blah blah about the band, and even break-ing into little chipped-off parts of songs. You and Daphne were watching her too; your arm was looped over Daphne's shoul-der and your eyes were stunned and dreamy, like spotlights had been shined into them.

Hey there, runt, you said. I got you something. You tossed it to me, a bendable tube that was filled with electric neon yellowish-green liquid.

It glows in the dark, Daphne ex-plained. They were selling them at the concert. You should have seen it, Ben. The whole entire audience was swaying and glowing in harmony.

To demonstrate, she grabbed my light stick and rocked from side to side, all spacey. Daphne was like that. I grabbed my stick back.

I haven't been to a concert in years,

Mom said, the first words I saw her direct to Lyle. I could tell she was hauling every pound of blame for those missed concerts up on Lyle's shoulders.

Then you should get out more, Lyle answered.

Yeah, no kidding, Mom shot back. If I want to, I sure will. She sounded kiddish and overheated. I knew if I'd talked like that, I'd have got warned to get some sleep or drink juice.

But Lyle just shifted his eyes to you and said it was time to drop Daphne back at her house. I offered to go with him, thinking he'd answer no and tell me to scat back to bed, but he nodded okay, and I zipped my jacket over my pajamas. You wanted to go too, but Lyle shook his head. It was plain that both you and Mom were sort of nervous of Lyle, but weren't going to do or say anything else against him, not then. You barely said good-bye to Daphne or good night to Mom as she drifted up-stairs.

Daphne sat in the backseat and Lyle didn't say a solitary word to her all the way to her house. He did walk up to the door with her, to apologize to her mom for keeping her out so late.

Now what, Ben? he asked on the way home.

A dryness filled my mouth and I couldn't crumble out so much as a single, even partway helpful answer. So we drove quiet together, until I managed to tell Lyle the only thing I knew for certain.

Rules don't bug me, I said. But with Mom and Dustin, I think it was the rule of not seeing the concert that made them want to go so bad.

I hear you, Ben, Lyle answered.

However it wound up, with Mom and Lyle not speaking, or you grounded, or Mom grouching on the phone to Grammie, I can't exactly recall. What I do remember is that my dumb old neon light stick only worked for that one night. By the next morning, the color in the tube had turned to plain yuck-yellow.

The only reason I put it in my desk drawer and not my trash can was because it came from you, and I didn't want to be caught without it, in case you ever asked.

When I get back to the motel room, Mallory's found a squirt bottle of some kind of cleaner and a rag. I lie on the bed and watch as she squirts and rubs the rag over little corners of furniture, making faces if the rag picks up the smallest smudge of dirt.

"Your room is only slightly less filthy than mine," she says. *Squirt, squirt. Rub, rub.* "In fact, my room had a big dead fly squashed to the window. On the inside. I had to call the front desk to get someone to remove it."

"I'd have gone in and unstuck it if you'd asked," I tell her.

She makes a face and says, "Eghck."

Lyle tries to unpack his suitcase, but Mallory bracelets a hand around his wrist and tells him it's safer to keep the clothes where they are. "Because there's a high chance of catching bedbugs."

"Even in the bureau drawers?" I ask.

"Dustmites, then," she answers, and she starts into a story about how Channel Five did a special consumer report where they ranked all the motel chains in the U.S. from cleanest to dirtiest. Or at least they tried to, but as it turned out, all of them were filthy.

"Not all of them," Lyle says.

"Every single one," Mallory answers in a voice that won't change its mind.

I ask if I can have some money for the pop machine in the hall and they both spin on me and say no. Then Lyle goes on about how bad pop is for a person's teeth and Mallory tells what sounds like a made-up story about how the fizzes in pop chew away the lining of a person's stomach.

You would have got mad, I bet,

listening to Mallory's story. She's just a lady version of Lyle, I bet you'd say. Full of her rules and set in her habits, probably wishes there was a GCA, too. And in a way, you're right. Even how Mal calls her voice mail and makes tiny little notes in her Filofax is exactly the same way that Lyle calls the hospital and makes tiny little notes in his Filofax. They make plans together, tapping pens against their chins.

"First the hospital," says Lyle. "I'd like to get going as soon as possible."

"Then we'll find someplace for lunch," Mallory adds. "And we'll want to go back later this afternoon."

"I've left Gina the number of where we're staying, in case she calls in for her messages," Lyle says, staring at the phone.

"Where do you think she is?" Mallory asks.

"Who knows? She's not at work, she's not at home, she's not at the hospital. She's completely undependable." And Lyle cuts his pen through the air like he's crossing Mom off a list of Dependable People.

Lying on the bed, I close my eyes and think about how you'd take all this attention. I didn't ask you to visit me, is what I bet you'd say. It's not my fault people are missing work and wasting time.

You'd say these things and you'd mean them, but I have a hunch that part of you wants us here, inside touching distance, even if you don't want to answer for it. I never met anyone with less need for people than you, but not needing isn't the same as not touching. It's how you've been since I met you; half on the run and half hoping for the rescue, but then never exactly happy with the attention that a rescue brings.

One mom gone was bad. Two moms gone was too many. There was a while when the news wouldn't stay with you, and you thought she'd be home at the end of the week or the month. It wasn't until you realized Mom left us for permanent that you got working on a plan to leave too.

Gina sent us a letter, you'd tell me as soon as I biked home. Last year, at the start of fifth grade, was when Lyle let me bike outside our neighborhood. I spent every afternoon that fall on your old Hotrocks six-speed, either coasting around town or exploring trails through Pinewoods, which is what it says it is, a stretch of woods, mostly pine.

You dragged behind me with your nose in Mom's letter as I walked around the kitchen, hanging up my jacket and hunting the cupboard for snacks.

She says the sky's better than a postcard. She says she doesn't need her electric blanket and she's sending it back. UPS. She says she learned how to make gazpacho. She says she's moving into a condo only a mile from the beach, and she got herself a job as a vet's assistant. She says when can we come out and visit?

Mom hates animals, I answered, except for it wasn't true, but I liked imagining Mom's new life as a big lie.

When are you going out there?

I'm not. She can come here, she knows where I live. Why, are you?

Hell, yeah. Soon as I get my driver's license. I hate it here. This stupid town. Gina's where all the action is. No wonder she got bored.

There's action here.

If there is, I wouldn't know. Dad's

learned more ways to say the word no than any other father in the neighborhood. If I have to hear him one more time—Not today, Dustin. Maybe next weekend, Dustin. We'll talk about it after you're finished being grounded, Dustin. . . . I'd be out of here in a second if I had choices.

You're making Lyle out to be worse than he is.

I get my driver's permit in six months. Then I'm taking off. Gina won't care. I wouldn't stay long, anyhow. Just till I made another plan.

You can't drive there. I mean, you could, but it would take . . . a long time.

So?

And you don't have a car.

Dogger says I can buy his car, cheap. I'm making real dollars at Pete's Pizza.

Lyle'll never let you go.

Lyle. Lyle'll never let me go. Shheeez.

He won't.

There's this expression, Ben? About how some people can't tell their ass from their elbow? Every time I think of that expression, it reminds me of you.

Up till that minute, it had been a regular you-and-me conversation, a bopping talk that wasn't exactly right and not exactly wrong, either, but instant and easy like playing tennis against the wall with me as the wall but I was used to it.

Except sometimes you hit too hard—you did then—and my wall fell down and there was no way to bounce back.

I stared at you, then lifted my juice to my mouth and drank it down in one long slow sip to the end.

It didn't matter what you planned, I decided. Just as long as Lyle and me didn't have to be part of it.

Lyle wants to get going to see you, and we're out of the motel so fast it's like we spun through a revolving door. Someplace between my run up and down the gravel hill I guess I lost my sweater, but Lyle doesn't notice and Mallory doesn't notice, and since it's warm enough outside that I don't realize I forgot it, there's nothing to protect me from the hospital. I start to shiver as soon as we walk into the lobby.

"Where's your sweater, Bennett?" Mallory asks.

"Forgot it," I answer, looking around

for a place to reheat. The top-down drive had been quick but liquefying hot, and I feel like I got hauled off the beach and stashed into a giant refrigerator full of sick people. They are everywhere, bumping their walkers or partnered up with nurses or sitting raggedy as missing socks in their wheelchairs.

"Third floor," Lyle says, coming back from the information desk. "Gina's up there already. Elevator or stairs?"

"Elevator," Mallory says, and we head to it.

A cold hospital layer is starting to cling over the heat in my skin. I'm hot/cold/hot in rings moving out and out from the pit of me, like a radar. The rings stretch out and out and blip to the third floor. I'm sweating and shivering, so I start to jog in place, trying to even out my temperature.

"You okay?" Mallory asks. "Bennett?"

And Lyle goes, "Ben? Ben?"

Whatever they say next I don't know because it's lipped-over-me words and I'm listening to the squeak-tap of my sneakers on the hard hospital floor. I'm shivering but there's sweat-prickers in my scalp.

Then Mallory has my hand and we're walking together, through the automatic doors, back into the sun.

"It's too cold in there," I tell her. "I'm not ready to go in there."

"We need to pause," she says. "You know, I haven't dashed around this much since I was a newsroom assistant. How about lunch? How about a cheeseburger or chicken nuggets, sound good, hey, Bennett?"

"Yeah, okay."

Lyle stays behind, so it's just her and me moving outside the radar range. Mallory's heels tick over the pavement and she jingles her keys in one hand, but her other hand snaps mine palm to palm, firm fingers through my fingers. Her sparkly nails scratch over my knuckles like I'm her pet Chihuahua, but it is enough, holding her hand and loosening up in the heat.

Once we're in the car, I feel better, and I ask if I can get a milk shake along with my cheeseburger.

Me and Mallory got off to a bad start, and we're still making up for it. The fact of us both trying to smooth things over I take as a sign that we'll come through all right. Lyle'd taken Mallory out a few times before, so when he invited her over for dinner, I knew it was a tester for Lyle to find out my opinion. Since Lyle works at home, he can spend the whole day fixing up a meal, which means a home-cooked dinner is not a bad idea, datewise. When I got home from school, good smells were thick in the air. I figured the night was kind of Mal's tester of me, too, and I even took a shower and changed into a button-down without being asked.

I'd already seen Mallory on TV, so her clicks and sparkles weren't a surprise. She was livelier than I'd counted on from a semifamous person, and her questions were easy lobs about school and friends; no curve balls to sneak me into talking about Mom.

Mallory's own stories took longer, and I switched on and off paying attention. The main facts are that she ran away from home when she was sixteen to live in Paris, France, where she was a clothes model for magazines. She ran into some bad luck when she married a creepy French guy who used up her model money. She divorced the creep and she finished high school by mail, and then she took newspaper-reporting classes at some Frenchy school. She moved here when she got a job to be the weather lady on a cable channel I never heard of. She did such an awesome job that the big cheeses at Channel Five wanted her do their Sunday Consumer Edition. She landed the weekend spot after Craig Calhoon went to another TV station out west.

That's when Mal got spooked and started going to Lyle. She figured everybody would think she couldn't do the real news since she'd been a model and a weather lady. She needed help getting the quivers out of her voice, she told me, and to learn not to bust up crying when she got angry, or if her boss got angry, or if people wrote in that they liked Craig Calhoon better. Which they did, at first, because nobody likes changes.

But she included too many extra ministories about big shots she knew in Paris, which of course Lyle thought was so, so great. He kept saying, You were friends with *her*? You went to a party at *his* house? Once, when he was in the Air Force stationed in Hawaii, Lyle saw Jack Nicholson in a gift shop. That was almost twenty years ago, and Lyle still talks about it. I guess to him, movie stars are like the super-confident polar opposites of the people he has to shake the shyness out of all day.

From Paris to Lyle, I said at the end of

the dinner, right before my favorite Lyle specialty, homemade peanut-butter brownies. And I don't know, maybe I said it because it sounded like something you'd say, a crooked insult you might have flipped me from when I first came to your house. Then I felt bad, because Lyle's face turned red and he started twirling his fork in his hand.

Ha ha ha, Lyle embarrass-laughed. From Paris to me. What's my special charm, Mal? I keep asking you, and see? Now Ben wants to know too.

Dessert didn't taste good after he said that. That's one of the ways you and me are different: you stand guard by your smart-mouth remarks, but I want to turn them around and march them right back up inside me.

Guess you never read a single chapter of *Speaking to Save Yourself*, Mallory said to me, hard-voiced. Otherwise you wouldn't poke fun.

Dustin calls that book the Bible for Babies, I said.

Lyle had cracked up when he'd heard Dustin call it that, but Mallory was wrong for the joke. She leaned forward, the points of her elbows pressed on the table and, with her chin socketed to her fist, checked me out long and hard, like it was the first real look at me she'd ever got.

Ignorant, she said finally. And I wouldn't have thought so, from a first impression.

The silence tingled my cheeks and sucked out my appetite. I pushed my brownie over to Lyle and then, turning a shoulder against Mallory, I told him how Mrs. Adams, our recess monitor, just came back from her honeymoon in Paris, and she said that the sidewalks were full of dog poop.

"**H**ow are you doing? Better, Bennett?"

"Better, Bennett," I answer, and because it sounds funny I repeat it a couple more times in an outer-space voice until I see it's kind of getting on Mal's nerves and she tells me don't talk with my mouth full.

"Thinking about seeing your mom . . . maybe it gave you a jitter jump?" she asks.

I plug in the last bite of cheeseburger before I tell Mallory that I don't care if I ever saw my mom again for the rest of my life.

"Liar," she answers. "Come on, finish chewing. You're a sorry listener, I swear, Bennett."

"I'm serious." Except for I can't tell if I believe it myself, since it closes up my throat to say.

Mallory sips her water and quietly says some words about Mom that Lyle might have cut her off from saying if he'd been here at burger place too.

"You never met my mom," I remind her. "You don't know what she's like."

"I know enough to form opinions," Mallory answers. "And however nicely you cut it, she's never been much of a mom to you."

Mal's right, I guess, but in a small way I think I should speak up for Mom. It's hard to catch up with all the different ways I think about her, even after so much time away.

"However nice you cut it," I say slow, "Mom couldn't have stopped Dustin from doing what he did."

"What are you talking about, stopped him? It was a mistake, what he did. An accident, Bennett." Mallory spreads her hands wide to heaven, showing me, I guess, how nobody could have caught you, how you'd fallen through everybody's helpless fingers.

"If you say so," I tell her.

Mallory's sunglasses are off and her eyes hold me to a better answer. Pretty eyes she's got, so dark that the white parts look like glow-in-the-dark decals. She leans her face in close, serious.

"What makes you think that Dustin would want to hurt himself?"

"He wouldn't want to," I answer. "He just would."

I t must have been some time right before or right after Mom left, that day we
took bikes out to Pinewoods. Your bike actually belonged to Lyle and mine was the
Hotrocks hand-me-down and neither of
them fit us perfect, but they got us around.

The race was your suggestion. We'd
biked into town for snacks, and you paid
for everything. My mouth hurt in a good
way from grape pop and two Eskimo Pies
and handfuls of jawbreakers.

Let's race, you said. Like a real race,
like a marathon.

I said sure, why not? because even though you'd win, it was a day when your whipping me on a bike wouldn't have made me mad. Not mad at all.

We shortcut behind the fire station and went off road. My bike frame was thick with knobby tires, better for the mud and long grass, and I couldn't figure how you kept balance on those ruler-thin wheels and hanging over your handlebars like you were. I had to pedal fast to keep up, and my box of jawbreakers, fitted between my belt buckle and my stomach, rattled like voodoo.

Pinewoods is bike land, with good trails and just enough rocks and hills to make you feel like you're Daniel Boone in the wilderness. Some of the trees along the trails are marked with red or blue or yellow dots. Blue is a good trail. Yellow cuts down a mountainside and is too steep. Red is for little kids.

You took yellow.

Dustin, I called. Hey, Dustin, your bike isn't going to let you. Yellow takes you all the way down the mountain.

Go red trail, then, you said, without

looking back. That's the safest. I'll meet you at home.

But I knew your challenge when I heard it. That inside-out, you kind of challenge. I switched gears and pumped strong, holding you in sight just barely, you were treading so fast and bouncing hard into the rhythm of every slope and bump.

Yellow tree dots blurred past. I tried to ignore them as I kept up speed. We were jagging sidelong down the mountain, which I knew only from Lyle's saying so ended somewhere over by the bakery outlet on the other side of town. Even with my hands triggered over the front and back brake pulls, I was feeling not-so-sure that I could stop myself if I needed. You weren't checking or warning me, tourguide style, about the rocks and gutters ahead. But I kept up and stayed quiet, my back pressed low and both sneaker laces coming untied and nothing to hear except the cracking twigs and *rat-a-tat* of my candy.

Your back tire caught the stick as you were skidding away from one of the pricker bushes that stuck up everywhere through the woods.

Dustin, your tire's caught, I called. Stop—watch it! You can't shift gears.

All my voice seemed to do was jump your speed. My eyes were trained down on the stick clacking through the spokes, and so when I raised my head, the shock gusted through me. There'd been no warning on the clean drop of mountainside that fell before us, steep as a ski slope and just as bare.

Dustin! I shouted. The sound of my voice made you pause without stopping, more like a hiccup between slow motion and freeze frame, and the next thing I watched you tip yourself straight down the mountain and let go of the handlebars, then raise your arms high like victory.

I braked so fast my stomach heaved. I watched as you waterspouted over your bike, which kicked away from you like a wild pony before smashing onto its side. Your arms and legs churned the air as you punched up extra height before the spit of the next instant knocked you all the way back down to the ground. It happened so quick I had trouble processing that it happened at all.

I ditched my bike and ran to where you had rolled, flat on your back with your eyes on the sky.

Why'd you do that? I shouted, collapsing to my hands and knees beside you. Why'd you let go? The dusty gold sunlight and creaky pine needles closed too calm around my thumping heart and questions. Still I kept asking.

Why? Why, Dustin?

You scowled as you inched up on your elbows. Maybe the bike got away from me, you said. Then in an undertow of breath, you told me someone called your name.

That was me! I was saying to stop, to get the stick out of your back wheel.

You nodded, but your eyes fixed steady on the ultrablue sky. You held yourself to the same position for so long I began coughing just to jump-start your attention.

Slowly you brushed yourself up to your feet and went to collect your bike.

I watched as you straightened her out and pulled the stick from where it was still lodged in the back-wheel spokes.

You did that on purpose, didn't you? I wanted to shout. You just wanted to test how it would feel to drop down. The only reason you did that was to see if you could, right? Right?

And jealousy itched at my skin, thinking of how good it must feel to fall so free, even while I could have punched you for it, for scaring me so bad.

I swear you must have read my thoughts when you turned and smiled, a goofy, tooth-filled clown smile. We were a pair, a pair of adventurers and close as real brothers, in spite of what you'd said before.

Hey, Ben, what's brown and sticky? You waved the stick in the air. Get it?

I laughed too hard and gave you some jawbreakers for the long ride home.

Mallory keeps asking if I'm feeling okay now, and I keep answering yeah, although I guess the day is starting to wear on me. I can't stop yawning.

"Wait here," she says as we drive up to the hospital. She ducks in and after a long time she comes back with Lyle and Mom. I'm glad I didn't have to be around for the Mallory-to-Mom introductions.

"Ben!" Mom yells. "Come here and give me a hug!" She holds out her arms.

I put my fingers on the door handle and then decide on second thought that I'll just stay put and let the hug come to me. Some of my shivering's back, and I'm not even in the lobby.

Mom looks different; her face is tan and her hair is lawn-mowed short. She's wearing a pink sleeveless shirt and pink globe earrings, and I realize you're right, her ears do stick out.

When I lean out of the car to hug her, I smell the mint off her chewing gum.

"What's on your arm?" I ask.

"Smoker's patch. I'm quitting. Well, I'm trying."

"That's great. Lyle says cigarettes'll destroy you."

"The Surgeon General said it first." The look in Mom's eye tells me that Lyle's warning wasn't the exactly right thing to come out of my mouth.

"Look." I stick out my wrist. "I've got on my watch."

She nods but her eyes barely move to it, and I think maybe I should have got out of the car and hugged her when I'd had the chance. We've started off on the wrong foot, Lyle would say.

"Your mother's coming by the motel

later, to take you out to dinner," Lyle tells me. "If that's all right by you, Ben."

"All right," I say.

"I've got a nice place picked out." Mom smiles. "Reservations at eight."

"That's awfully late for dinner," Lyle says.

"It's all right," I say, and Mom says, "No, it's not," both of us answering Lyle, but it sounds like Mom's answering me, and then we kind of laugh and Lyle says, "Hey, do what you want," in a voice that doesn't really mean it.

Mallory slips into the driver's seat and uses too much engine noise revving up.

"Let's get going," she calls. She glosses on some glimmery lipstick and checks her sunglasses in the rearview, being Very Special, but I know she's just edgy, tripped up in the tangle of all these wrong-footed starts.

I try to climb into the backseat, but Lyle stops me. He squeezes in the front and pulls me over his lap.

I'm way too big to sit in people's laps, but I figure since we're so far away from school and nobody will see me, I'll let him.

Mom crosses her arms to her chest and steps up on the curb and looks at us in the car. "Wow, regular little family," she says, and she sounds so all alone, I half-wish somebody would say something to make her feel more included. Nobody does.

Mallory vrooms the engine again. "Nice to meet you, Gina," she says in her anchorwoman's voice.

"I'll pick you up at seven-thirty," Mom says with eyes on me only. "We're going someplace really special, my favorite restaurant just for you, Ben. So wear a coat and tie."

When Mom was ready for a move, I knew her symptoms. I had a head start on you and Lyle, since it was all the same stuff as Before. The afternoon naps and long walks, the waking up or coming home at dinnertime with eyes red-simmered from tears. Or she'd go out shopping for hours and return with a foot massager or new wineglasses or an atlas. Weird stuff. Same patterns that made me mad and careful both. I didn't want to topple her mood by asking her about it, but I didn't want her to think I couldn't tell she was restless and straining to go someplace new, someplace where her old problems wouldn't find her.

One afternoon, I'd caught her staring out the kitchen window with eyes more hopeless than they should have been from a view of recycling bags and tomato vines.

It's so difficult, she sniffled when I made myself ask her what was wrong. I guess I'm just a difficult woman. I guess there's just no pleasing me some days. . . .

You used to say that Before, I reminded her. Every time, before a move, you would say that to Dad.

Maybe you're right and maybe you're wrong, she answered, kind of absentminded, like right or wrong didn't even matter.

And Dad followed you wherever you went.

Frank's a follower by nature. I wish Lyle—

Lyle's lived here a long time. He won't go anywhere else, I said. And me neither, I almost tacked on, except for I couldn't. Instead I asked her if she wanted to get back with Dad.

No, no, Mom answered. What's past is final. It's only lately I wonder how right I am for here. There's got to be more than some little nothing nowhere town, some little nothing nowhere life.

Well, count me out, I almost said, trying again. But the words were too Aquaman soft for the power of the feeling trapped inside me. What I said was, Guess I'll go up and do my homework.

In chapter five, "Relax, Recall, Respond," of Lyle's book, there's a diagram of a person with arrows labeling the abdominal muscles and diaphragm and trachea. If you want to get your words out right, Lyle's book explains, then all these parts of your body have to be unrestricted.

In the bathroom mirror or on the bus, I practiced unrestricting myself, preparing for Mom.

Lyle's house has a backyard and a waffle maker. My room is the exact right color blue, I told my reflection. I watched my teeth and tongue and the movements of my lips and I practiced saying whatever came to mind. I'm in my third year at the same school. My fort's here, in the branches of the same tree where I carved BEN. It's my secret fort, where I stash my compass and the naked lady coasters I took from King Plaza.

Besides, Lyle's not going anywhere. Not. Going. Anywhere.

Relax, recall, respond. It's all about keeping yourself in charge of your thoughts and throat when the tension turns high. Lyle's main point is that you can't squeeze up or you'll run out of air. That breathing is everything.

So I was ready for her, that night when she came into my bedroom to give me her piece. She sat at the foot of my bed and rested a heavy hand on my leg and began to talk like she was telling me some baby bedtime story, a story about leaving for a while, just her and me, getting out of this little town to see the world. I kept my palms flat over my abdomen and measured the slow fill and drain of my breath.

When she was through, I sat up.

Mom, you'll have to go alone. The words growled deep from the cave inside me. Because I'm staying with Lyle. I've lived here longer than I've lived anyplace else, and now it's my home. It's where I'm from.

Ben, please. There's not a chance I'd ever leave without you. You're my own son. We're on the same team, right?

She was restricting, though. I could hear it perfectly, nasal pressure. That's a warning in Lyle's book. Nose talking means nervousness.

If you want to be with me, you'll have to stay here, I said. My throat was as unrestricted as a python about to swallow a mouse.

Watch your rudeness, Mom told me back, clenched and sharp. Don't you talk to me like that. But then she kind of sagged, as if a lead ball had rolled to the pit of her stomach, and I knew she was feeling unfixed on everything—her plan, me, and who was really on her team.

She sat there on my bed until I told her, Okay, good night.

Still she sat, trying to think up what to answer. Except for all there was to say was good night, which she finally did, quiet and through her nose.

111

I knew there'd be more, and there was, but not that night. That night, all she could do was stand up and walk out, scared off by the sound of the voice Lyle gave me.

"It won't make a difference if I wear one or not," I tell Lyle, but he grumbles.

"She does this for attention. Gina sets up these silly obstacles," Lyle says to Mallory once we've pulled onto the highway.

Mallory doesn't answer.

Back at the motel, he keeps jawing. "I never knew Gina to walk into a coat-and-tie restaurant. Fast food, that's what she loves. Fried chicken, fried fish, French fries, fried—"

"Okay, enough." Mallory shakes her head. "Let's put an angle on the positive.

For one thing, there are shopping malls everywhere."

Lyle frowns and slaps open the side locks of his suitcase, pushing through everything in it. "She knows we wouldn't pack a tie, let alone a . . . a dinner jacket!"

Mallory looks over at me and winks. "You sound like you could use a nap," she says to Lyle. "Bennett and I are going to check out that pool."

"No, no," says Lyle but then he puts his hands on his eyes, like he's testing out how a nap might feel.

"We'll wake you if we need you," Mallory says. "You're exhausted."

"She's right," I say. Lyle looks yellow, the last-week-of-a-bruise color. He thinks on it and then agrees, but only if we wake him up in an hour.

"We're out of here," Mallory whispers as soon as we're both walking outside. She takes the car keys out of her pocketbook and clinks them together. "If I had to hear that man go on one more second, I swear I'd have popped him a knuckle sandwich."

"Where are we going?"

"Shopping, of course."

It's my second trip of the day with just Mallory, and I mention something about that.

"Yeah, we're good together, you and I, Bennett," she answers. "Although for the life of me, I don't know what we have in common."

I'd been thinking on that, too, and I have an answer ready. "We speak out of our stomachs and say what we mean," I tell her.

First Mallory frowns like she doesn't understand, but then her eyebrows push up over her sunglasses as she nods her head, and I know she gets it.

Liptwitch gives us directions to a department store, which we find easy. Soon as we walk through the sliding doors, Mallory's got everybody snapped to attention. In ten minutes, I've sampled more shirts and jackets and dress pants than I ever wore in my entire life.

Mallory says my hair and eyes need a vibrant palette. She uses lots of Very Special words like that, and both of the sales guys eat it up.

Finally, we go with a tan sports coat

and navy pants with a white shirt and a navy-and-red striped tie.

"You don't have to do this, Mal," I tell her as she hands her credit card to one of the sales guys.

"Bennett, have you ever owned a sports coat that wasn't handed down from Dustin?"

I think on that, and the answer seems to be no. "See, I never had much use for one," I begin. "Dustin's ones always fit enough."

"There's this saying," says Mallory, and then she tells me some scrambly French words that sound like *say-bluh-wuh-kwa-plyoo* or something, and I wish I knew French.

"Yeah?"

"It means, it's only the first step that costs. Times like now, you've got to own yourself, Bennett. It's my pleasure to help you feel like you're not just anybody in somebody else's jacket. But the rest is up to you. When you see your mom tonight, it's up to you to know who you are. And I'd start by ordering the most expensive thing on the menu. It'll give you some nerve, and nerve lives right next door to courage."

None of her advice is from Lyle's book, so I know I'm getting a free page out of the real Mallory. "I know another expression, in English," I tell her. "It goes, the clothes make the man."

"Ah, that's a good one," she says, but I have a feeling she heard it before.

She crumples the receipt into her purse so I won't see it, which is nice of her. I know if I'd caught a look at the total, it would have made me feel weird.

Every good time I spend with Mallory feels like another handful of loose change dropped into a rainy-day water cooler. If hard times ever come up between her and me, there's some genuine savings to fall back on.

"Is saying my whole name Bennett part of owning myself?" I ask her when we're driving back to the motel.

"Mainly I like the sound of Bennett," Mallory answers. "Especially when you consider that everyone and his brother is named after the guy on the hundred dollar bill."

It takes me a minute, and then I tell her that's a good one.

Even before your permit came through, you were driving Lyle crazy. Counting down calendar Xes to your permit and driving his car around the block without permission and saving your pizza money for Dogger's half-wrecked car with the taped-up back window. All you could talk was car, car, car, and when you weren't talking car, you were so quiet you seemed invisible.

How did that paper turn out? Lyle would ask you. The one you were writing on the French and Indian War?

Mmm. Your face bent over your dinner, your chin an inch from the table. As soon as you were done eating, you'd ask to be excused, polite enough so Lyle had to say yes, but quick enough to show how much you didn't want to stick around.

More than once, Lyle got called in to talk to your teachers about your cutting school or, when you did show up, your bad behavior. Wild pranks like spray-painting your locker or deflating the basketballs in the gym with your black–T-shirt friends. And since there wasn't a mom around, I got the bulk of Lyle's worrying.

What should I do, Ben? he asked me more than once. He refuses to stay in counseling. Punishments, rewards, fear tactics—nothing fazes him, nothing interests him.

It's probably a stage, I'd usually answer, which seemed to be the most settling explanation, the one I'd heard the most on television talk shows.

All you really wanted was to visit Mom. You wore Lyle down with the asking.

Gina can't handle you, Lyle would say. She's trying to work out her own life.

But Lyle couldn't handle you either, and once you got your license and bought Dogger's car, there wasn't much anyone could do to stop you from leaving.

You took off on the Fourth of July, while Lyle and me were at the town fireworks, and you pulled up at Mom's two days later. All the way across the country, nonstop except to refuel. When you phoned us from her place, it wasn't any surprise. Lyle had figured where you'd gone, and he'd already wired Mom extra money to pay for your visiting expenses.

Lyle's always been a think-aheader.

Mom said she'd take you for the summer, but that was it. You'd have to go back once school started, she said.

How you got her mind changed is still not all the way clear in my understanding, but I bet it wasn't too hard. Mom always had someone to keep her company. First Dad, then me, then Lyle, now you. A fair trade so long as I got to keep Lyle, I figured. All truth told, I didn't mind hogging Lyle for myself. No more sharing.

Lyle wasn't exactly as pleased. He fussed and fumed and even went over to

Dogger's, poking at him with questions about how long you'd been planning this, why didn't you want to live with us, why wouldn't you come home. I could have told him Dogger wouldn't have the answers, at least not the ones Lyle was looking for.

Tell Dad to get off my case, you said to me, calling collect when you spared it the thought. Tell him to send my transcripts so I can enroll here, otherwise I won't go to school at all.

He wants you home.

I'm here now. Gina's going to phone him any day, soon as she gets around to it. There's two bedrooms, so she's still got her privacy. She told me it was okay. Besides, I met this amazing girl, Steph, and she's teaching me windsurfing.

What about Daphne?

What about her?

There wasn't anything to answer. I figured if you didn't want Daphne, you didn't want anyone, since Daphne was the person you tolerated the easiest. And of course, Mom came to your rescue. In a letter to Lyle, she said that living in such a small town all your life, she expected any-one sane would go mental.

Your mother is making a statement at Dustin's expense, Lyle said as he handed me the letter. That was the first time I ever heard him say *your mother* in that bad, my-fault way.

But he transferred your school records. Both sides lose in a contest of stubborn-ness, Lyle explained, and Dustin will come home when he needs me.

Maybe Lyle really believed it, maybe he was just talking to persuade himself, but the fact that you'd be back soon wasn't the kind of thing to question Lyle about. Not right then, anyway, when missing you was like mud on his heart.

"**W**ell, get an eyeful of you!" Mom says when I meet her in the motel lobby, doing a sort of pop and spin away from the dingy glass sliding door where she'd been studying her reflection.

I go to hug her at the same time that she tosses me a small, silver-wrapped package, which I have to step back to catch.

"What's this?"

"Something small. A nothing thing. You look really great, Ben."

I shrug my shoulders but I feel not too bad, especially after my long shower and

Mallory's comb-out of my hair. She even knotted my tie a special Frenchy way.

Lyle hadn't been as helpful through the time of me getting ready. He just kept going on about Mallory spending too much money, even though I told him it was her pleasure. I wished I could have tossed out that slippery French expression about how only the first step costs. That would have fixed him.

But when Mallory was done, Lyle softened up and said that he didn't even recognize me. Which is how Mom is looking at me, too. I'm not one for liking the feel of church clothes, but when I saw myself in the mirror, it was something. I could have passed for a teenager.

"You can open that now, or anytime," Mom says as we walk out to the parking lot.

But the present turns out to be weird, a bracelet made out of rope. A girl present. I look at Mom for a couple of seconds to see if she's kidding, before I say thanks and slip my hand through.

"It's soft," I tell her. There's not much else to say.

"It's a friendship bracelet. Everyone out here wears them. It's all natural, made out of hemp," Mom explains. "You can make anything out of hemp. Shirts, anything. It's wonderful."

"Okay," I say, but then I tuck the bracelet behind my watch, out of sight. It doesn't go with my sharp Frenchy look.

"Do Lyle and his lady friend have dinner plans?" Mom asks as we get in her car, a small buggy car, the kind she always likes to drive.

"Her name's Mallory. Chinese takeout and pay-per-view," I answer. "But first they were going back to the hospital to check on Dustin. He was asleep last time."

"Lyle mentioned that you weren't ready to deal with seeing him, earlier."

"Hospitals are creepy," I answer. "You have to be a hundred percent ready for them."

"Hope you feel a hundred percent ready to see me," Mom says, flashing me a kindergarten-teacher smile and turning on the radio, which is set on a good hits station.

Just this afternoon, I'd told Mallory

how I didn't care if I ever saw Mom again for the rest of my life. She'd called me a liar and she'd been right, because actually it's not bad at all to be with Mom, sitting in the front passenger seat of her buggy car and listening to a good hits station. It reminds me of old times. We sing along with the music and of course Mom knows all the words.

The restaurant is far away and made out of glass and different from any other place I've been. First thing I see is a waterfall splashing into a pool right in the middle of the room. It makes people's voices echo into a big waterlogged noise.

Mom is wearing a red dress with white dots on it, but other ladies are looking show-offish, too, in tiny skirts and tall heels. Everywhere are fat guys chewing steak or cigars, and the piano singer lady is practically topless. The whole restaurant could be described as super fancy in a rated-R way.

"Your eyes are saucers," Mom says as we sit at our table. "You'll have to do a better job not to stare." She wriggles in her seat. "Isn't this funsie?"

I try to recall if I ever heard Mom use that word *funsie* before, and I decide no.

The waiter brings us menus and Mom says, "A nice bottle of red to start, please." I'd forgot about Mom and red wine. She used to drink it every night, even with fried-egg sandwiches.

When the wine comes, Mom toasts to how grown-up I look and says how I remind her of Dad.

I tell her that I can't really remember what Dad looks like anymore. "I haven't seen him since fourth grade," I say.

"He's been no kind of father." Mom's eyes get mean. "Old Frank. What a burnout."

"He sends birthday cards with money in them," I say. "And he calls me on Christmas."

"Oh, throw that one at me." Mom's laugh is out of tune. "Last Christmas I was on a boat in the middle of nowhere, Ben. There weren't any phones."

"I wasn't comparing you two," I tell her. And I don't think I was but maybe I was.

We go quiet as we read our menus.

The prices aren't listed next to the food, so I have to guess what's the most expensive. I figure it has to be the shark. I bet sharks are hard to catch. I also ask the waiter for some sweetbread to start, in case the shark tastes bad.

Mom barks out laughing when she hears my order and calls me a brave man. She orders a steak filet and takes a lot of time explaining to the waiter how she wants it cooked.

After the waiter leaves, she starts right in, telling me about the vet clinic and her scuba and how the weather here is good for her sinuses. I am sort of listening and also watching the restaurant people. It's the kind of place where you might expect some gangsters to show up and start a shootout. In fact, there's one guy at the table ahead of us who could pass for a gangster no problem. Could even be a gun in his side jacket pocket. Gangsters call it packing heat.

"And I counted, Ben," Mom is saying. "Isn't that awful? But it's true. Eighteen months. It made me want to cry."

"What?"

"That we've been apart for eighteen months. Ben! Haven't you been listening to me?"

"Maybe I can come see you this summer," I tell her. "Like if I have some free time after scouts camp, unless Lyle wants to rent that cabin upstate. Last year he did, I told you about it, right? How it was on a lake and we rented canoes? But if we don't do that, I'll come over here to visit you and Dustin. Okay?"

"Don't put yourself out," Mom says, sarcastic. She looks into her glass and swirls the wine around. "I've always imagined a special bond between us, a mother-and-son bond," she tells the wine. "I gave birth to you, Ben. You can't break that bond, no matter how long and far you stretch it. I've been good at not pressuring you to come out here. Very good, I'd say, since you're mine by law. You don't belong to Lyle. That's why I want you to think hard when you reconsider living here with me, your own mother."

I budge in my seat and don't answer, although I want to ask her how could I reconsider something I never considered in the first place? But that would sound too smartmouth.

So instead I say, "Well, it was fun singing in the car and all."

Mom's eyes go a little moist then, and her hand reaches out to close around my fingers. "Tell me. Have you forgotten Before?" she asks. "When it was you and me, or even with Dad? There are days I miss, when you were little, when Frank knew how to have fun. Don't you remember all the fun we had, us three?"

"I don't go back that far," I explain.

Then the waiter struts over with Mom's salad and my sweetbread, except for it's not sweetbread at all, it's some kind of meat mash with gravy splattered on top.

"I didn't ask for this," I say to the waiter and Mom, whoever will listen.

"Sweetbreads, sir," says the waiter, and he nods his head at the mash. The way he says *sir* sounds like he's making fun of me. Then Mom tells me the disgusting truth that sweetbreads are another name for baby calf brains.

"Someone could have told me that

when I ordered." My voice isn't so polite. Mom smiles away the waiter, then leans over the table candle, gritting her teeth so that her smile becomes a pretend of what it was. She looks like a jack-o'-lantern.

"Is this how Lyle's raising you? Lord, at least you could try the food that you ordered and that I'm paying for."

"There's no way I'm eating baby cow brains. That's obscene."

The restaurant smoke is tingling my eyes, and the waterfall words and plinking piano are drowning the thoughts in my head. I squeeze my eyes shut against the smoke sting.

"You are unbelievable," Mom says. "I take you to this beautiful restaurant and all you can do is sulk. You're a real prince."

"It's not my fault," I say.

"Oh, it's mine, then? Are you blaming me? Go ahead and order something else, whatever you want. Double my bill. See if I care."

"I don't want anything. I don't need anything from you." A few people are looking over. "In fact, here. You can take your stupid bracelet back, too." I pull it off my wrist and toss it into her salad, where it lands like a giant onion ring.

"Great, Ben. Congratulations. It only took you twenty minutes to ruin this evening for me."

And I know she means it, too, and so I decide I'll ruin it all the way.

I stand up from the table, push back my chair, throw my napkin over the brains, and tell her in as unrestricted a voice as I know that she better drive me back to the motel.

Right. This. Second.

I told Mom I didn't go back that far, but I'm lying. I remember too much of my Before, same as you. You used to talk about your Before, always plunk in the middle of some wrong time, like during our first Thanksgiving together.

Remember Before? you asked Lyle, just as him and Mom and you and me sat down at the dining room table. Remember Before, when my mom put horseradish in the mashed potatoes, how good that was? That was like the perfect way to have potatoes.

Lyle answered something easy on everyone, a nice thing about your mom's cooking and then something else about how a real Thanksgiving always should have mashed potatoes, and weren't we lucky to serve some up now?

The harm was done, though. I felt the ghost of your mom glooming in the shadow while we said grace and passed plates. You made me see into the Before room, when it was just you, your mom, and Lyle. A perfect Thanksgiving.

I didn't have those rooms in my Be-fore. Mom and Dad were eater-outers, all the time, even Thanksgiving, when one year they found a seafood place that was open for an all-you-can-eat Thanksgiving special on beer-battered clams and shrimp. Back then, Mom's hair was down to her waist, and she had to keep pushing it be-hind her ears to stop it from getting in the tartar sauce. They made me wear a bib even though I was too old, but then Dad tied on a bib, too, and Mom was laughing and saying, Frank, quit being a bozo, just this once?

Then Dad and Mom went out on the

dance floor and didn't come back. They danced and another guy was dancing with Mom too, and Dad would grab her away, and they'd dance over to the bar and refill their drinks while I sat at the table and chewed and watched them.

There were some little pink packets in a holder on the table, so I opened them and poured the white powder all over my shrimp. At the time, I didn't know it was sugar substitute, all I knew was the powder tasted awful, a million worse times sweeter than sugar and it shriveled my tongue like salt on a slug. It's a mystery to me why I kept on eating. There was no more water, so I drank some of the wine from the bottle, and that tasted awful too.

After my stomach turned sick, I tried to hide it by throwing up under the table. The waiter who found me there scooped me up and carried me into the restaurant kitchen and gave me a glass of seltzer and a roll.

Oh, Ben, Mom said after the waiter found her, too, and brought her into the kitchen to reclaim me. She picked me up from where I was sitting on the floor. She hugged me hard and kissed my head.

Oh, Ben, she whispered soft. Why do you always have to go and ruin Mommy's fun?

The drive to the motel is full of the radio music turned up too loud. Mom doesn't talk to me but she does everything quick and huffy, even the way she taps her fingers to the music and snicks on and off the turn blinker.

Lyle answers the door wearing his pajamas. He is holding a Chinese food carton.

"You're back early," he says.

Mallory is in her pajamas too. She's sitting on one of the beds and watching the television. Without turning her eyes away from the screen, she hands me a carton of

Chinese along with a fork rolled into a napkin. "Fried rice," she whispers.

"Sorry for dropping in on your evening," Mom says, "but Ben decided to end dinner prematurely."

Instead of answering to that, I walk over to the farthest-away chair in the room and sit down and start eating. I'm starved.

"What happened?" asks Lyle.

"Thuh," says Mom through her teeth. "What didn't happen? Let him explain. I'm dead on my feet. I'm going to the hospital at eight tomorrow morning. Will I see you there?"

"Sure," agrees Lyle. "Around eight, eight-thirty."

Mom's voice drops, but I hear her tell Lyle something about how she doesn't envy him.

"Your loss," Lyle starts, and then I can't hear the rest because it's too quiet, but whatever he says, it makes Mom leave quick.

After she's gone, Mallory stands up and yawns and tells us good night. She leaves for her room, and so it's me and

Lyle. I move to sit in the space where Mallory was, next to Lyle, and watch the television alongside him. It's a movie I saw before, but there's something good tonight about seeing a story where I know how it ends.

When the movie's over, Lyle goes over to my suitcase and gets out my pajamas, which he hands me along with a new toothbrush still in its box.

"In case you forgot yours," he says. "I went to the drugstore, earlier."

When I come out of the bathroom, he's in his bed, reading. "Better get some shut-eye, sport," he says. "Another long day tomorrow."

"You should probably report me to the GCA," I say. "Because I didn't act so great at dinner with Mom."

Lyle puts down his book and takes off his glasses, then cleans them careful with a corner of his sweatshirt while he thinks out what he wants to tell me. "Your mother is still growing," he says, in the serious voice he uses to talk to clients. "One thing I'm sure of, though, Ben. I'm sure better days lie ahead for the two of you."

"She wants me to come live with her."

"That choice is all yours," Lyle says. "It always has been. You know that."

"Maybe when she's finished growing," I tell him. "Not now. I'm good where I am. Okay?"

"Okay," answers Lyle, and then I hug him good night quick before I climb into the other bed. He turns off the light and soon I hear the swing of his sleep-breathing. It takes me longer, could be since it's not my own bed, but prickly sheets and a slab of motel pillow.

Somewhere in Lyle's book, there's a section about concentrating on some kind of happy time from the past, to help clear the mind. It's another relax-exercise for before making a speech, but I use it for falling asleep. I always go to the same one, too. A summer day from a lot of years ago, when Mom turned on the lawn sprinkler of one of the houses we'd lived in, I don't remember which one or where. What I do remember is how the sprinkler moved like a giant waving water-fingered hand, and Mom and I ran back and forth, back and forth, in and out of the spray, trying not to get too splashed but wanting to feel the scatter of cool drops on our skin.

That mom doesn't have much to do with the person whose time I keep ruining, or the lady Lyle sometimes calls *your mother*. She is shaped and colored shadowy from being inside my memory for so long, and her voice and her laugh and the smell of her clothes might never have happened the way I invent them in my head. But it's how I stay near her, the best way I know how to hold her close.

he hospital is still cold the next morning, but I'm prepared. I've got on my sweater that I reclaimed off the gravel hill, and over that I'm wearing my new sports jacket. Plus I'm perked up from the carton of orange juice Lyle bought on the way over.

Mom lurches over and hugs me when she sees us in the third-floor nurse station, but her hug falls apart quick, to show me she's holding a little grudge from last night. I knew she'd be that way, but still it feels not so good.

"The nurses are changing his fluid

142

bags," she says. "It'll be a few minutes."

We wait around without talking, but as soon as the nurse signals us into your room, everyone gets noisy, ringed around your bed and smiling and asking how you're feeling.

I join in, but you catch the fear in my face.

"Big Ben's freaked," you say.

"No," I answer, except you're right. I hadn't expected the skinniness of your arms or the leathery black-and-blue shiner that fills one side of your face.

Everyone's drizzling over you with words about the nice nurse and the nice food and your roommate, Mr. Anthony, who is at X-ray now but who is nice too. I can't stop staring at the tubes in your arms and the bandages holding you in at the seams.

I lean against the window ledge, next to a vase of flowers that Mom says were sent by the people at her vet clinic. The flowers are rubbery and sun-bleached at the tips. Nothing like what people would send back home. Nothing that would cheer me up or make me Get Well Soon.

Then Mallory says she's hungry. "Is anyone else hungry?" she asks.

Lyle and Mom say yes and I say yes, but Lyle says, "Why don't you stay here with Dustin, and we'll bring you something from the cafeteria?" and I realize it's kind of a plan for me to spend some time alone with you.

"You look demolished," I admit once they're gone, which makes you smile. You have Lyle's face, I realize. Stiff edges, soft in the middle.

"I feel better than I look."

"How long are you in for?" I move closer, aiming for the chair by your bed.

"Doctor says a week, and then some outpatient therapy. I'm trying to figure if they'll let me go early for good behavior. Take a chair, if you want."

So I sit.

"What's with the getup? It that what Dad's girlfriend makes you wear?"

"Mallory? No. No, Mal's okay."

"She's a fruitcake."

"I thought you'd call her that," I say, "but she's okay. She's sort of famous, actually."

"How?"

"On TV. She does the news for Channel Five. She's not bad."

"Gina's asked for a divorce. I don't blame her, considering."

"You can't blame him, either. My mom was the deserter. Not Lyle."

"'My mommy deserted me,'" you say, imitating my voice but making it sound stupid. "You could have come out here anytime, you know, Ben. I was the one who had to fight for it."

"There's nothing out here," I say. "Everything important is back at home."

You don't answer, but you're breathing quick through your nose. Inside its purple cave of skin, your eye slides back and forth like a trapped black ant.

"How come you stay here, anyway?" I ask. "Your friends are always asking me about you."

"I made new friends. I like it here, besides, Gina lets me do what I want. She always did."

"That's not really the job of a mom," I say, and I wait for you to say something mean, to imitate my voice or whatever.

You don't. You turn your head. Your good eye is peeled and stuck wide open looking at me, surprised. "Well, I got gypped out of my real mom," you answer, "so I take what comes my way."

"Lots of people get gypped," I say. "My real dad's gone and my real mom's gone too. I got gypped, right? Right?"

"You can't compare yourself to me, runt. It's an insult. My real mom died. Who died in your family?"

I don't have anything to say to that, so for a minute we just breathe at each other like two boxers, and then I take a swing. My breath reaches for its strongest place. "You're out on the beach all day," I start. "That's what you told me on Thanksgiving. You must know all the good diving points."

"Yeah?"

"Which is why I'm wondering if you did it on purpose."

"What?"

"Your jump. Everyone thinks it was by accident."

"Of course it was by accident." Your eyes, good and bad, move to stare at the ceiling. You've gone back there, I figure.

High up on those rocks, watching the sky.

"Like that day on the yellow trail, in Pinewoods. How you pushed off your bike."

"Or maybe the bike just got away from me. Maybe I slipped."

"I always wondered what that must have felt like, to push off."

"And maybe this time I slipped too," you say, your voice turning hard, locking me out. "How would you know why I do what I do? How would anybody? I'm sick of people trying to stamp answers on me."

"Forget it then. Sorry."

"Just because people have questions doesn't mean answers come attached."

"Sorry, I said."

"Nothing to be sorry about." You yawn, too wide, and stretch your arms. "Anyhow, I'm tired. Go be with Gina. I don't want to gyp you out of your time with her."

"I'll go if you want."

"Yeah. I'm tired now."

And so I stand up and say, "See you later."

Just as I'm about to close the door, I

take another chance. "Dustin, I hope you come back and visit Lyle and me, even if there's nothing important at home." My throat sticks a little and I try to unrestrict. "Because Lyle misses you, you know. It's not like I'm a replacement or anything."

You don't stop looking at the ceiling. "Right," you say. "I know that, Ben. But I appreciate your saying."

I close the door and keep my hand on the knob, wondering if there is anything else to tell you. Waiting for the elevator, I almost turn around. I almost turn around and run back to your room and say how bad I feel, taking away all those things that didn't belong to me, like your work space and Lyle, even your outgrown sports jackets and your Hotrocks six-speed, when I couldn't trade for anything good.

When all I could give you back was the wrong mom.

But I don't turn around. The elevator opens, and I step into it, and I guess I will just have to live with that.

That afternoon and the next morning, when we come back to say good-bye, I'm always in a group. No more you and me. But the talking feels easier when more people are standing by, helping each other out of the silence traps.

Lyle's got you promised to fly back for a long visit in the summer, except for I don't think anybody except maybe Lyle believes in it. You go on about how you'd love to eat another Pete's Pizza and to tell Dogger you'll see him soon, but it's mostly just conversation air whipped up to fill the corners of the last hour before we leave.

Outside the hospital, Lyle talks to Mom about therapy for you. He asks her to send him the bills. Mom listens mostly, but she also reminds Lyle about how she can't make you do what you don't want.

"Dustin's a free spirit," she says, and I watch Lyle's hands fist up in his pockets. I watch him rock up and back on his feet. Annoyed. Pent up. Maybe even wishing he'd never set eyes on Mom that day in the Stop & Shop.

"I'd give anything to have Dustin under my own supervision," Lyle says. "But if he won't come home, you've got to help me here."

"I'm no miracle worker," Mom tells him.

"He's out of my reach," Lyle says.

"Join the club, pal," Mom answers, tipping her head to where I'm standing beside Mallory's car. "I didn't ask for this arrangement either. Welcome to the modern world."

Lyle's next words are too low, since he knows I'm listening in. Probably, though, he's telling her something easy on everyone, something about how he knows Mom will do her best and try her hardest. Hoping that by saying it, he'll help make it come true.

Me, I want to go. I've seen enough of motels and hospitals and restaurants. It's time to head home.

"We never used the pool," I remind Mallory as we're checking out at the front desk.

"It was septic," she answers. "I wouldn't have let you near that water." When Liptwitch overhears this, she looks like she might start crying.

This time on the plane we sit together with Mallory shared in the middle. Lyle passes out gum to keep our ears from popping.

Mallory asks for her Very Special stuff—a clean blanket and a twist of lime in her water—and she gets the plane man apologizing for everything but the weather. Either Mallory has totally memorized Lyle's book, or she never needed much help speaking to save herself in the first place. Still, she was the right person to call. She is the right person to sit between me and Lyle.

The movie starts and I've bought earphones, but Lyle and Mallory bend their heads together and continue their conversation about you that has no way to finish. Not that day and not ever.

Halfway through the movie, I fall asleep on Mallory's arm and I don't wake up until we're touched down, safe on the planet again.

The last time you came to see us was the Christmas right after you started college. You were taking classes in marine biology, and everything seemed to be going great for you. You brought your new girlfriend, Elise, and Mallory had to pretend she needed to go the grocery store, only she really split off to the mall to buy Elise too many presents, wrapping them in the family room with the television turned up loud so Elise wouldn't hear the last-minute rip of scissors and tape.

Next we heard you'd left school and

were living one place, then other, but always drifting around the coast. Some bad words between Elise and Mom had broken you and Mom apart, and so the faint news of you that had trickled through Mom ran dry. The magnet of whatever pointed you home rubbed off slow, until nothing pulled you back our direction, not even holidays, not even Lyle's wedding to Mallory that you promised on the phone you'd make. You were Lyle's best man right up to the last minute, when I stepped in and took your place.

When we got the news, I never doubted for a minute that it wasn't at least partly on purpose, although no one saw you, and no one even knew you were gone for a while after. Lyle went out there by himself this time, and came back looking partly erased. The fact of it takes me by surprise, even now. Who would have thought there'd be so many not-yous? Under a hat or across the street or next to me in line at the movies; I'm always just about to call your name. Sometimes I do.

The hardest part about your leaving is that whenever I think back on our Before,

I can't find what I need there. The kinds of memories I keep thinking I owed you, or that you owed me. It hurts to realize that I will never remember you in an easy way, a comfortable way, now that your unsettled life is finished.

But when Mallory lights a candle on your birthday, I find you in the blue hot flame, and see you the best way I know how. You are standing high and straight, your shoulders square against the wind and your eyes lost on the distance. I watch your body flicker and sharpen and fall through the air to the water, hardly rippling its surface as you disappear beneath it. It's how I stay near you, how I keep the best of you with me.

Besides, you probably would have called it the perfect dive, if you'd spared it the thought.

In memory of
Jason Berg
1971–1997